Altogether Elsewhere

Anna Wilson

Published in 2003 by Onlywomen Press Ltd, London, UK.

ISBN 0-906500-77-X

British Library Cataloguing-in-Publication Data.
A catalogue record for this book is available
from the British Library.

Typeset by Cynthia Fayers
Printed and bound in Great Britain by J W Arrowsmith Ltd

ORDER OF DOCUMENTS

ELSEWHERE: ONE

A picks up a brick, throws it through a window. Her spirit rises with the brick as it flies through the air. What joy, an inrush of oxygen, as the glass splinters. That noise, the awful suddenness of it, how it lances into the brain. A knows there is nothing like it, as she runs her feet are lighter, her strides longer, she can run forever.

Only later does A worry about what throwing a brick means, what she can achieve with each brick. Who is it she really wants to throw a brick at? Soon her mind is full of faces. She sees her past, now, in terms of those people who didn't get the brick they deserved. A worries, that her anger has come to be so personally directed. Experimentally, she goes out again, choosing her favourite, most delicate-coloured brick. She writes 'beware' on the side of it with an indelible marker. In the earliest hours of the morning she throws it through a clear expanse of glass. As she runs through the streets her head is dizzy, dancing. She can run forever. And yet, sleepless the morning after, it is not enough. She doubts the morality of the act. Whether it is fun or not is not really the question.

A goes to visit her brother with a brick in her suitcase. She lies in bed at his house staring at the ceiling. She remembers how he used to have power over her. Do this if you want to be my friend, he used to say, put your hands there. At the time it was easy, to put her hands where he said, to move them as he directed. It was only later that she felt abused. A lies in bed, remembering. Take that, she mutters to the ceiling, feeling the hard brick under her pillow. She takes the brick down to breakfast in a plastic bag, thinking that she may throw it into her brother's porridge. Did you have a good night, his wife asks. Much as usual, A replies, putting away her brick.

A carries her brick back home, gazing longingly at the windows of the train. But prudence restrains her. And she is still doubtful as to whether she ought to be throwing bricks, if it is only for her personal satisfaction.

A realises that she does not want to abandon the throwing of bricks, that her life would be the poorer without this intoxicating sensation. She reads newspapers, looking for a solution. One day she sees in the paper the account of a violent attack. The accused defends himself: the woman was drunk, he says, and strangely dressed. The judge condemns the man's use of excessive force and recommends future restraint. He hands down a suspended sentence. A reads the story over and over. She cuts out the story and pins it on the door of her refrigerator. Each time she bends down for milk, she meets it eye to eye.

A begins to keep her ear to the ground. Soon she finds out where the man lives. She goes to visit his house, passing it more than once at several times of day. A few days later she returns, carrying a brick, on which she has written 'beware'. She throws the brick, letting it soar through the air. It passes over his hedge, over his little garden and through his living-room window. The glass tinkles and breaks, a high-pitched noise. A draws in her breath, watching the beauty of the brick's flight. She flees on light feet, floating on a pure, clear exhaltation.

A has found her vocation. She is no longer assailed by doubts. Each brick she throws she throws not only for herself but also for the common good. She scans the papers eagerly for new targets; almost every week she throws another brick. Eventually, someone makes a connection: a particular kind of violence brings with it the risk of a brick through the window. The streets are uneasy. There is always the fear, they say, that someone may be sitting in its path. What if it were to strike the tropical aquarium? A's activity becomes a part of the language: "A brick is all you deserve", the women say to their men, dismissive. A notices, gradually, that she is not alone. Women are everywhere with bricks in their hands. A smiles to think of those others, running through the streets with oxygen in their brains.

✳

SOURCE MATERIAL: GLORIA

'I had to wash Gary's shorts.'

I bet you did. Gloria opens her eyes, 'Why, did he have a little accident?'

'He has them almost every day, Mrs Johnson.' Belle plumps a cushion with sudden vigour, 'I wouldn't say that he's toilet trained, myself.'

'I think he has the general idea.' Gloria smiles, sunny.

'It could be that he's disturbed.'

Gloria hitches Gary up onto her hip, 'Well, jesus, he's not the only one.' She is out the door before anyone can say any more and fleeing down the stairs, Gary bouncing.

Belle stares out the street door after her, these women think they're doing you a favour. Always the bus is late, the boss locked them in the cupboard, them clean clothes fell in a puddle on the way over. They think you're stupid, the stories they tell. Belle steps back, letting the door close, stares vacantly through the blurry patterned glass. That Gloria, she's in too much of a hurry.

At the corner Gloria pauses, looks down at him: 'Just don't shit in your shorts 'til we get home, that's all.' Gary grins and folds his hands about the strap of her shoulder bag. On the bus, in a crush of people, Gloria braces her feet apart and sways, Gary and her bag heaped to her breasts. The traffic stands, inching forward and grumbling. Agile unencumbered youths swing on and off the platform, eyeing the stop ahead. Gloria's legs throb wearily. It is no surprise, a shock only, to feel a hand search across the flesh of her thigh. She turns with difficulty in the crush, cannot tell in the layering of eyes that look elsewhere, gathers herself: 'Somebody's feeling me.' Loud above the dull thud of the bus. Gloria looks them over, who are trying so hard not to see or hear. She thrusts Gary out suddenly, at a man gone red-grey: 'You want to feel this nice warm shitty baby instead?' Gary wails, thrust into space like a bag of rotting fruit. The crowd shudders. An orange escapes from some shopping bag and rolls along the aisle, rubbing at ankles. The man moving hastily away from Gary steps back and crushes it pulpy underfoot.

✷

This Sunday morning, sleep leaves her. Takes up residence somewhere else. He sleeps on, works hard at Saturday night's pleasure. Gloria stares into the corners of the room with prickly eyes.

At seven, Gloria rolls her way out of bed. Today only the light-hearted wrap will do. Its gay pink elephants are creased, there is a sock in the pocket, but it's the good times wrap. Sitting on the patio pretending it isn't three feet of rotting concrete in what passes for summer, eating cherries. The not quite getting dressed all day because there's really no need and no one's in the mood to care, wrap. Just the thing for this cold dawn when the only thing to be said for it is that she's awake in it alone.

She shuffles down the corridor. The door to Gary's box has swung to. She opens it, always half afraid that he hasn't enough air, shut tight in such a small space. He has captured a chiffon square, yellow in the street light, under his cheek.

Next door Grace has propped her door open, as though she wouldn't hear Gary half a street away. As though there was anything she might miss about Gloria's return, lumpen and sighing, in the middle of the night. Gloria looks in, expecting her eyes open, ready. But she too asleep, the sleep of the overworn, curled and desperate.

Gloria glides back up, squirrels herself behind the kitchen door, turns on the lights. What's this then, a carnival, blazing awake and all alone. She puts the kettle on, looks in the fridge. The same territory, always half-eaten cans of pineapple, a peanut butter sandwich Gary forgot. Gloria pokes about, an anarchic hope forming. Finds a paper bag, in the end, hidden clever behind the frozen peas, no man's land. Cakes. Gloria peers in, four: him, her, Gary, Grace.

And now we have to consider what is the right thing. Gloria sits at the table, nursing her cup of coffee. Finds herself apostrophizing the Lord. It's a Sunday morning, after all, and the training lies deep in you. At first blush, Lord, there can be not much doubt about it. What decent woman would so much as contemplate the consumption of the little Sunday treat her aged mother has bought. The intended centre-piece of the table on a nicely patterned plate, four bright-iced cakes. We can almost imagine that Grace has been wearing out her tired, old eyes on the weaving of a lace doiley to go underneath. Except, Lord, that they will fight unseemly about who's to have the chocolate one or maybe today some other colour, for who knows it's all random and to do with the weather and makes no difference so long as they all for sure will want the same one. Whereupon there will be a further little contest between Ma and I as to who can make the best martyr this day. Or else he will take the carving knife to them and cut the whole lot into little pieces. Eat up your spoonful of coloured rubble, Gary, and quit crying. Gloria rocks back in her chair and lifts her eyes to the ceiling. You know, Lord, I am not altogether sure I can face this scene. Maybe you have something else to suggest, like that I should go for a long walk by the canal and fling myself in, leaving them a spare cake.

Gloria squirms in her chair. It is ridiculous that there is nothing comfortable to sit on in the kitchen. If she had an armchair she could go to sleep in here, would never need to leave. She lifts her feet up onto the table. Well, oh fluffy blue mules, and how is life with you? Did you imagine yourselves on me when you came out of those factory gates? How did it feel when he put you down once and for all on the counter and shelled out, and you faced your destiny on my feet? Gloria reaches out and tweaks one of the mules. It springs back into shape, leaving a faint wrinkle.

Gloria takes her feet off the table again, wearily, reaches for the coffee jar. Feeling exactly how she would expect after no sleep and a night spent in the prowling of this city's uncouth streets. Give us a lift, Lord, or a cake at least.

She stands at the window, looking out over the yard. Two broken chairs and that tricycle he had imagined not past mending, illuminated by an attempt at dawn, no sky down here, only its most muted effects. Like so many other things, that we do not seem privileged to obtain at first hand. Gloria is a woman deserves something, surely, on a sleep-free Sunday morning, having carried herself about the streets looking for other women's troubles so that she may put herself in the way of them. Being a barrier, that must be worth something?

Gloria reaches a plate from the cupboard. A pattern of interlacing strawberries. She takes the cakes out of the bag, arranges them gently. Listen, Lord, I know this may not accord with your view of things. You are accustomed to making us wait one hell of a time for our reward, and if it comes along it has a tendency to be something more spiritual altogether than cake. You are accustomed also to a good few sacrifices along the way, such that if I want to eat my son's cake or my husband's cake I must stamp right on that desire and divide my own cake between them by way of suitable recompense.

Gloria sighs, tired. The ritual statement of what she ought surely to be doing weighs heavily. But there seems little doubt that she is about to commit this act of betrayal, the consumption of the cake.

There they are then, square, iced, their sweetness palpable. Gloria seats herself at the table, examines at leisure. She removes from her mind the question of the rightful destination of these little artifacts. What the mind's eye don't see. She looks at them with a view to considering which she is going to eat first. It is a choice, girls, between the pink and the white. As so often, indeed, we are only reflecting life itself. As Miss Hudson remarked, you, Gloria, may play a chocolate drop. I think Louise makes a more suitable sugar plum fairy, don't you. I do, of course. We will eat the pink cake first in memory of Miss Hudson and her supporting cast of chocolate drops. Gloria's teeth close upon the limp pink cake, collapsing it in seconds. She eats it in two bites, quite a hunger got up now with all this waiting and justifying.

Gloria licks her fingers and grins. She glances; there is no one in the doorway. A fragment of icing has melded itself to her front. She spots it away with a precise finger.

Once begun upon the feast, the joy of indulgence has begun to build, intoxicating, within her. Who needs the light of day with one down and three to go and the Sunday silence unbroken. The white one now, the disposal of it is only a duty. They do not quite have the face to make the sponge inside dead white. In case someone at last notices there is something nasty about it, bleached flesh. Gloria bites down, a hatchet job this, a kindness to put it out of its misery. Away with the little cake of absence.

We are getting along just nicely now, the hard work out of the way, the dawn up and over with. Gloria yawns and moves the two remaining cakes into line. The yellow with that twist of fake peel, its tiny hint of sharpness. It makes an effort to amuse, this cake. And the brown, her ordinary self cake. They lean together against the empty strawberry pattern all around them. Gloria hesitates, and lingers. You see, Lord, how much satisfaction I have obtained from the following of my own inclinations. To some of us it might suggest that things might be better if we were to do this more often. I hope that you can trust me to fulfil my obligations. Because without trust we are surely undone. There is no point in my talking to you at all if you don't trust me. Gloria pokes at the chocolate cake with her finger. It falls onto its side, exposing the soft naked sponge of the underbelly. Gingerly, Gloria rights it, her tongue squeezed between her teeth. To thine own self be true. She picks up the yellow cake, smiles at it, and bites it in half. She crunches its peel, its small zest, carefully. The half-eaten cake in her hand springs back into shape. Usefully elastic. Like her blue mules, manufactured into resilience. Hard wearing. Happy lemon cake to have found a stomach with an eye to your qualities.

Gloria feels mellow, sugar bliss charming its way along the bloodstream. Uninterrupted by hunger, merely for unalloyed pleasure, she is about to launch herself upon the not least but last, the saved for savouring, cake. When Grace appears in the doorway, dragged from her bed by this dancing Sunday morning act of defiance.

'I just had a feeling about those cakes.'

Gloria jerks in her chair. She draws her wrap around her, endeavours to compose herself.

'Lord knows, I did not purchase those for your own little breakfast.'

'Blessed is the giver, Ma.' Gloria's glance flicks sideways, her hand comes to rest casually upon the edge of the plate.

Grace shrugs: 'Go ahead, I'm not stopping you now.'

She watches intently. The chocolate cake goes down, the focus of all attention. Gloria eats it slowly in three distinct bites. As she licks the crumbs from her lips and leans back Grace lets out her breath, a sharp hiss. They look at one another across the room.

'I can hardly believe the evidence of my eyes.' Grace's gaze sweeps across the kitchen, revelling in the gift of this depravity, such a scene.

Gloria rises, gathering herself for the exit. The departure from grace with a fling of her pink elephant-strewn wrap, nothing she can't take in her stride today.

*

The laundry is warm in winter, at least. The summer of course, it is warm also. Rivulet weather. Now don't go dripping on the shirts, girls. No one makes the chargehand wear an overall, she parades her dinky blouses. The customer doesn't want to know how you perspire. Gloria peers through the glass, she's out there now, sweeping her way through the shelving, finding someone to blame for that lost tablecloth. In the almost quiet of the office Gloria kicks off her shoes.

'Finished yet Gloria?'

'Not yet, Mr P.. Dividing all these big company profits fairly between everyone, that takes time.'

He retreats back into his office. She is always peevish on Fridays.

Flat-heeled sandals on the concrete outside. Kath opens the partition, closes it crumb tight. 'Someone's whipped that tablecloth, I can smell it. Who do they think they're kidding.' She leans over Gloria's desk, 'Mrs May was going to have a party, wasn't she? Big do.'

Gloria lays her arm across the cards, against Kath's lust for others' secrets, 'Big tablecloth, I suppose?'

'Oh, well, isn't that what they always say. My grandmother's priceless damask, it's not the kiddie's bib they lose.'

'Just give them the twenty quid, who's bothered?'

Kath folds her arms. Her green washed-out eyes flow over Gloria, 'Funny sort of wage clerk you are.' With the same knowing resignation she watches out the corner of her eye, as if waiting for a tell-tale flash of creamy damask.

'That little Nasneen, isn't she going to have a baby?'

'Then she's going to wrap it in a tablecloth.' Gloria bends down into her desk drawer, brings out the cash box. She puts it in front of her and folds her hands in her lap.

'I don't know. She might wear it. What do I know about these people?' And she is out the door, in pursuit.

Mr P. looks at the totals, weighs each packet in his hand. He likes to have an intimate knowledge. Gloria waits, abstracting herself from his interest. She considers her fingernails; it is years since she bothered to paint them. What colour would that be, now?

'How's Mrs Teale making all this?'

'There was a lot of pressing.' A delicate peach perhaps, two-tone effect.

'Hope she doesn't get used to that style of living.' He pushes the box over, 'Better go and lighten their lives, then.' He watches Gloria out onto the floor. He likes to stand, seeing them hide their little packets away in secret places. Hands fumbling, eyes blandly elsewhere.

Grace sees her coming, stacks the fancy iron on its end with a clang. 'Takes you longer by the week.'

'He likes to finger it all first.'

Grace takes her packet, dropping it neatly down the

front of her dress, 'Maybe I should go back on the piecework.'

Gloria riffles the pile of blouses stacked at the end of the board. Flimsy, with frills: 'When you can put your soul into these?'

Val is leaning her head against the great juddering drum of the washer, puffing smoke into the steam. Gloria waves across a great waste of water and throbbing sound. Val pushes herself upright and sloshes across, 'You brought my reason for living?' Gloria grins, 'Got any spare tablecloths?'

Val unzips her coveralls, 'Underneath this lot I'm naked. Like to see?'

'You should get a transfer. The isolation is getting to you.'

'Ah, it's got to you, has it. The office is sanity now.' Val walks backwards through the water until her head is resting on the drum, her body shaking to the machine's rhythm.

'Here's looking at you, Glo.'

✱

Gloria throws packets of tea into the bottom of the trolley. Gary leans towards the jars, just out of his reach.

'You want tea, Ma, don't you.'

'Grace opens her eyes wide, 'Sure, I couldn't live without it, could I?' She rocks from one foot to the other, a little dance for Gary in the supermarket. Her dress shimmers brightly.

Gloria's mouth folds into a line. Her feet hurt.

Grace darts off down the aisle, her eye lighting on the packets of instant dessert. She picks up a green one, turns it over in her hands, 'I could maybe fancy one of these.'

Gloria, hurrying to catch her up, pushes the trolley too close to the shelves. A cascade of packets, multi-coloured, fall into the trolley, over the floor, into Gary's lap. Gloria and Grace bend to pick them up. Grace's hands are quick and accurate, her fingers nimble. Gloria crams battered packets back onto the shelves. Grace make a neat pile, bright as building blocks, in a corner of the trolley, daring Gloria to deny her.

Gloria wrenches a packet out of Gary's mouth, 'What you want with that?'

She plunges off toward the check-outs. Almost there, she sees out the corner of her eye that Grace has not followed. She turns around. Grace is waving across the store; Gary laughs. 'You missed this whole aisle.' Grace gestures at a long tunnel of delights, 'See? Canned fish and dried fruit and so on.' She peers over her glasses at the label on a tin of salmon, 'I expect it's tiring, pushing that heavy trolley about. And of course you're carrying more weight on you than I am.' Gloria opens her mouth, shuts it. Decides she had best simply admire this deliberate energy that stands up in the face of a hostile world and will not be defeated.

Grace's hand hovers over the sardines, 'There's so much to choose from, isn't there?'

Outside the diner Gloria stops to shift bags from hand to hand. Before she knows, Grace and Gary have homed in, conspiratorial, on the chrome and pastries.

'I think we ought to stop for a cup of coffee. You look so tired.' Grace perches herself on a high shiny stool, wrapping her legs about its stem.

'I wouldn't mind something to lean on.' Gloria puts her elbows on the table.

The woman behind the counter flicks a rag across the plastic:

'That'll be the day.'

'You want a chocolate doughnut? We're having one.'

Gloria drags her cup towards her, 'Your teeth'll fall out.'

'Lord knows, you can be difficult, Gloria. Why so joyless?'

Gary looks down from the immense height of his stool and grips his plate too hard. It slides towards the floor and he sways and rocks.

'You want to fall off?' Gloria grabs a handful of his shirt.

Grace runs her finger round the edge of her plate, 'For

what we have received.'

'I don't suppose you remembered the washing powder.'

Gary makes a leap for her lap across the yawning chasm.

*

They are almost at the end of the promenade. It is not clear quite what has made it necessary to walk this far.

The bench creaks when he sits down. He grins at it, reproachful.

'You don't need to tell me, you bench. You think this is something I don't know?'

'Maybe it can't take the two of us.' Gloria feels the hot slats with her hand. Brittle, flaky green paint scatters across the pavement.

He waves it away, 'What the hell, sit down, we're on holiday, aren't we?'

They sit looking out over the sea, soundless with the roar of the arcades behind them.

He glances at her, 'See something out there?'

'Either you do Joseph, or you don't.'

'Well, and maybe I don't.' He leans back, lacing his hands behind his head.

'I didn't say there was any obligation.'

'That is a relief, now.'

Gloria takes her eyes away from the sea, looks at him: 'Why don't you walk on a little way Joseph?'

He glances along the path, at the few straggling shops, their yellowing beach balls, 'I think we already came too far.'

He leans back, searching for relaxation. Gloria follows the waves, trying to imagine that she can hear what they sound like. Perhaps in a small boat, out on the water.

Joseph opens his eyes, 'We must look just like everyone else for once.'

'A regular black family by the seaside.'

'Nothing wrong with that.'

'No, Joseph, there isn't.'

He gestures at her, 'Then why you have to do this other thing?' He waves his arm at the sea, 'You go out looking to be different.'

They are silent, sitting together on the bench.

'Ordinary human achievement isn't enough for you.'

'Ordinary human achievement?'

'Gloria, you know what that means.'

'I know what that means?' She turns herself to face him, 'How do you know what it means for me?'

Joseph gets to his feet, a long way from the depths of the bench to his full height. He looks down at her: 'If it was ordinary, like everyone else, then I would know, wouldn't I.' He turns away and begins to walk down the path, back towards the milling sand.

He is almost out of earshot, 'I thought you approved of my beating up those guys.'

'Well, maybe you were wrong.' Joseph proceeds into the distance, reclaiming Gary and Grace hoarded somewhere in the far-off morass of deckchairs.

Gloria watches him go, neat yellow and blue sports shirt, long stride. Full of his wisdom. She knows what he is expecting: succour and faith, to be shored up by her unbending belief. Her duty in this white world, is she arguing with that?

She is not on holiday, after all. Wherever she goes, she must think the same thoughts. Maybe Gary is on holiday, he is thinking about sandcastles and where to put his flags. So long as nobody interferes, he will be away. Different places are different to him. She turns her shoulder from Joseph, looks out again over the pebbly strand.

Gary has crawled under the chair. The convex dark round of Grace's arse looms over him, a great weight almost touching his neck. He crouches, head pressed between his knees. From under here he sees legs – going past, stopping – but always without any clothes on. He has time to examine them; sometimes they stand still, sagging, for minutes at a time. They seem larger than ever, a pair can take up the whole field of his vision, he has sometimes to turn away from the size of them. Gary watches them, unseen. If they go on standing in front of him it comes over him to want to touch them. Grace stirs in the heat, her hand flops over the side of the chair. Gary twitches and shifts his position, not to be crushed. There is a paper flag in the sand between his toes. Gary picks it up very gently.

Gloria is playing games, little jokes with herself. Why would a woman like you, practical, she asks, have these ideas. These ideas, the cobbling together of a boat, sailing due away from this slum oily channel of water. Just her, just her and Gary, though she'd have to take them all, not wanting to arrive there without family. Ma would be sure to have cousins. Gloria finds herself noticing an old white woman shuffling along the promenade, her knees gone by the look of the way she walks; it brings her back to a northern resort town where cleansing tidal waves, hurricanes and the like are not often seen. Gloria smoothes minutely the crease in the strap of her sundress and sighs.

Gary reaches out, flag held by the very end of the stick. The square of paper quivers. With a sudden jerk he prods forward, into pink calf. The legs twitch and Gary compresses himself into the shade. The legs loom larger, turning ponderously in a circle. When they come to rest at last Gary holds himself back, biting his lip. He holds the legs motionless under his gaze, denying them movement.

Gloria picks absently at the bench. Long shards of paint have lodged themselves under her nails. The afternoon is taking its time passing, has become a thick soup through which she must swim. For no reason but that she has found herself in it, her arms moving rhythmically to keep herself afloat.

Joseph has just changed a bank note into very small change, which he is feeding piece by piece into a machine. At any moment, he reasons, a huge tottering pile of coins will cascade over the cliff into his arms. Something, at any rate, is bound to happen soon.

Gary gathers himself and lunges. The stick buries itself briefly then falls away, leaving a sudden whiteness across the leg. The beach seems to scream, a fraction after, and there is an unlooked-for upheaval above him as Grace lurches out of her seat. Gary squints up into the sunlight.

'He stabbed me, your little boy.'

Grace's hand flicks out. Gary covers his ears, 'Didn't mean to.' The hand stops, just a fraction away. She wasn't going to hit him for a thing like that, but pink legs doesn't have the eyes to tell the difference.

'I don't know what you was doing under my chair.'

'Shitting, Granma, you look.'

Grace walks round the deckchair, expectant.

STREET SCENE: ONE

Elsie twitches the curtain aside and looks out into the scrubby winter garden. She had given up cutting the grass when she realised that she would never sit out there in a deckchair, reading the Sunday papers. It was not the kind of thing that went on in that garden. It surprised her that such an image still lay trapped somewhere in her mind. Looking at it now, she sees men in uniforms leaping over the walls, converging, large boots squashing the hillocky grass. She sees them clearly, superimposed on the darkness; only a matter of time.

The first key turns in the front door. Elsie feels her shoulders stiffen; automatically she checks the garden again: not surrounded.

'It's me, you know I'm always early.' Tam throws herself into a chair, 'Make me some coffee, Elsie, it'll be good for your nerves.'

'You would be nervous, in your house.'

'You think I'm not, out on the streets.'

Elsie sighs, pouring water into the coffee pot. Mama waiting at the gate, hand raised against the sunset. Waiting for her own little gangsters to come home. Welcome little ones, I was so worried. Aw, Ma, don't you fret. She sees the young blade's contempt in the lift of Tam's thin shoulder.

She sets the tray down on the floor, 'I take risks too, that's all.'

'Lady, could I forget how you suffer?' Tam takes a mug gently from between Elsie's short, pink fingers.

The rest arrive then, together, a rush of dark clothing and the cold of the outside air. Elsie pours more coffee without looking up, clenching her teeth against resentment, watching Tam's long dark hands fold around her mug.

'Anything happened? Anyone notice us?'

'I've read the papers. Nothing special in the local.'

'Same routes, then.'

Elsie focuses on Sue's exotic ski gloves: 'We're not in this for the excitement.'

Gloria smiles at Tam across the room: 'Just shows how we blend in with the background.'

‘These white folks are conspicuous.’

‘But subtle,’ Sue says, easing a zip home.

‘Don’t worry, Elsie,’ Sheila lays her arm across Sue’s shoulders, ‘Sue isn’t going to do anything silly. She wouldn’t dare.’

‘Time to go, Tam,’ Gloria says, touching her lightly, ‘ain’t it’. Liz and Ruth sidle out together, silent.

‘One two three four five six little gangsters.’ Elsie closes the door behind them.

In the underpass, Sheila flattens herself against the damp concrete, Sue beside her. ‘Your damn blonde hair,’ she says.

The woman is walking fast, the sound of her heels echoing high and uncertain. The figure behind her lengthens its stride, reaches out. For a moment she screams, and Sheila launches herself from the wall.

Sue has the woman on her feet, gasping, touching herself.

‘You’re all right, we’ll walk you home.’

‘I don’t know what I would’ve done.’

Sheila tests her knee, aching again, ‘You would’ve hit him.’

Tam and Gloria are walking through rich country, high walls and not a soul on the streets. It accentuates Tam’s anger; no one here had better ask her help.

‘You do know, don’t you, that if anyone gets done for this it’s going to be us?’

Gloria smiles, ‘That has always been the case.’ She speeds up, to get them away from there: ‘But it’s a good way of getting back, isn’t it.’

Liz and Ruth stand under the railway bridge, their backs against the wall. Liz moves her shoulders inside her jacket, ‘I don’t know why we’re doing this.’

‘Maintaining a presence on the streets.’

‘And then what?’

*

He has his window wide, elbow trailing over the sill.

'Never laid black arse,' he says, smiling.

'Look Gloria, greymeat in a Cortina. Isn't that nice.'

'What an opportunity.'

Gloria kicks upwards into the joint of the elbow. The car swerves across the road, quivers, and straightens.

'That could've been a nasty accident.'

'Though I say it myself.'

They have walked all night without incident; the streets are silent but for the hum of the street lights. Only the cold moves, coming up through the soles of their shoes.

'This is a waste of time.'

Though Liz is relieved at the quiet, that she has not had to test her reluctance.

'Maybe we've made the streets safer already.'

'Don't be stupid, Ruth.'

'Joke.'

Ruth has no answer to despair, a luxury she feels that she cannot allow herself. If she were to stop doing this, her life would not be any more bearable.

'It's more difficult for me, when can I make up my sleep?'

'Sam doesn't look after the baby?'

'He thinks we should play happy families on a Sunday, the three of us.'

In the shadow of the gasworks they turn for home: Elsie's light discreetly on behind flowered curtains, tea and warmth. 'Why did I want to take hold of something outside?' Liz mutters.

Ruth spreads her hands, sighing.

'Who convinced me the real world isn't at home?'

Ruth shuffles along wearily, wishing briefly that she had a lover or a best friend, could climb into her bed and babble until dawn all the unspoken horrors of the night.

'The real world's gone out to a party in a pink rouched ballgown,' she says, knowing herself unheard.

Ruth props herself against the table, watching the

piece of toast that quivers in her hand: 'Still shaking.'

Liz has just left, putting down her tea and going with an unfocused wave of the hand.

'Something get to you?' Tam digs her knife into the jam.

'Only the cold.'

'Should kick the down and outs off the air vents.' Sheila hooks a chair under her and eases painfully into it.

'Seems a shade ruthless.'

'Yeh, not what nice girls do. Sue's learning, aren't you? Look at her eating fish paste like she didn't know St. Tropez from shit.'

'So who's heavy tonight.'

Sheila shrugs. 'All right. My knee hurts.'

Ruth buries her hands in her pockets, 'I'm going home, then. Coming?'

Outside a crumpled cardboard box scuds down the road. They walk slowly. Ruth listens to the sound of Sheila's indrawn breath. Outside Sheila's block they stop.

'Goodnight, then.'

'Is your lift working?'

'Shouldn't think so.'

'How're you going to get upstairs?'

She grins. 'One step at a time.'

Ruth pushes into the hall. 'Get on, I'll give you a piggyback. Lesbian lift service.'

'Oh, you think we should stick together, do you?'

At the top Sheila slides off her back, keys already lifted to the lock. Ruth leans against the damp, marred plaster of the corridor, breathing.

'Thanks.' Sheila pauses, looking at her sidelong, 'I'm not going to invite you in.'

'Don't mention it.'

Ruth start off down the stairs, breakneck, her feet making the stairwell echo. Sheila closes the door quickly, as if she had almost let in something dangerous.

SOURCE MATERIAL: SHEILA

Across the carriage, two boys talk about joining the army as officer cadets. Sheila rests her hands on her knees. The woman reading the morning newspaper raises it higher to obscure her face.

The boy whose hair falls across his face says, 'It's essential to get into the best regiments. I have the right connections.'

Sheila turns over the palm of her left hand and stares down into it, blank. The yellow, calloused flesh quivers with the swaying of the train. Despite the gloves, grime is ground deep into the lines of her hand, melded around the nails.

'I don't want to earn my living,' says the other, who knows nothing of regiments.

'No, it's very boring, isn't it.'

Sheila turns her hand over once more to clasp her knee. She balances the weight of her aching body carefully but without thinking, elbows flexed. She closes her eyes and moves with the train from side to side.

On the seat opposite the woman folds her paper into a short truncheon and clasps her handbag under her arm. She gets out at the next station, slamming the door behind her. Her place is taken by another carrying baby and pushchair. Sheila opens her eyes as the baby squalls.

The boys lift their voices over the noise, turning angry blue eyes at the mother. She rubs the child's stomach and murmurs. The seat beside her is piled with discarded layers of clothing. A gust of wind splatters leaves against the window: Sheila shivers, involuntary; leaves. Her mind is full, should she look for only a moment, of leaves piled, scattered, burning. Down at the depot the year's leaves are burning. She feels each shovel of leaves gathered from the gutter in her back, along her shoulder blades.

The baby quiets and the woman lifts her gaze.

The boys change trains at the junction, throwing themselves onto the platform.

Behind half-closed lids Sheila watches the process of inspection. The flickering stare that takes in her stained blue coveralls with the red city department brand, that lowers to her shoes, heavy and high-laced against the mud, that lingers on her face with furtive intensity. The baby has started to cry again, bleakly.

'Got a stomach-ache, has he?'

The woman starts, her hand ceasing its mechanical rubbing motion, 'Yes, I think so. Ever since this morning.'

'Got far to go?' Sheila smiles widely, harmlessly.

'Oh, no – nearly there.'

Sheila nods and turns her head politely away to look instead into the back yards of houses where, not seeing her staring into their kitchens, they will not be disturbed.

The woman lifts the baby to her face and presses him to her.

✵

She sweeps her broom in long arcs, a single stroke from shop-front to gutter. At the corner she pauses, leaning. A cold wind leaps at her from the side road. The shops are just opening, clanging steel shutters, pushing back metal windows. The blind violinist occupies his usual spot, tucked into the entrance of the supermarket. It is too early to play yet, so few passers-by and those, hunched against the wind.

He hears the scrape of Sheila's shoes as she comes to a halt, pitches his voice accurately across the pavement.

'Cold today, then.'

Sheila grunts, glancing sideways at the case lying at his feet. There are, as usual, just the two strings stretched across the bridge of the violin.

'Still saving for that new string.'

'Too old for g-strings, I told you,' his wickerwork stool rocks under him as he laughs.

They both turn their heads as a gust of wind picks at something in the roadway, sending it clattering to the curb.

'What's that?'

Sheila walks over and stoops, slowly: 'Just a lipstick.' She picks it up, turning it in her hands.

'You'll be able to use that, then.'

'What?' She pulls at the top and turns up the lipstick. It is a deep, dark red, hardly used.

'It's your lucky day.'

Sheila rolls the dim metal cylinder in her palm. Then she closes her hand over it and slips it into the top pocket of her coveralls.

'That's right.'

She begins to wield the broom, sending clouds of dust down the street in front of her.

✷

She wakes with that faint feeling of unease in the pit of her stomach that indicates the wind is up, battering the block from side to side. A moment later she hears it, hammering against the window. The sky moves past at speed, as if it will run out. Sheila gropes her way to the window; below her the snow glimmers in the dark of the morning.

The radio claims that all train lines are blocked, that the city's transport system is immobilised. Sheila joins the queue outside the telephone kiosk, who breathe steam through the scarves over their faces. They stamp their feet and kick the ground. In the kiosk someone lights a match to unfreeze the coin slot. Sheila pulls her cap down over her ears, against frostbite.

At the depot, no one answers. Sheila attempts to imagine rows of deserted street-cleaning carts, and no one shouting and banging around them. The all-night cafe is open, a crowd clusters round the open-air counter, their faces lowered towards cups of coffee. All the radios are tuned to the same station, giving weather reports and transport bulletins. They say the power lines are going down in the south-east sector.

It is daylight by the time she turns back into the entrance of her block, yet there is still little movement on the streets. Her neighbour on the ninth floor passes her, nodding, and dives off across the road towards the store.

For hours she plays patience, wearing an extra layer of clothing. At the end of each game she gets up to look out of the window; as the day wears on only the light changes. There are a few people out on skis, bent over against the wind. At lunchtime she goes out again to the telephone. The deputy manager answers, his voice is high-pitched.

'What are you ringing for?'

'You don't want me to come in?'

'What for, exactly?'

'Sweep the streets, maybe.'

'This isn't the time for brooms. Why don't you go back home like everyone else and leave me alone.'

Sheila shrugs her shoulders inside her coat: 'And to you, too.'

'I have enough problems.'

He cuts the connection; or perhaps another line has gone down, pulling out switches across the city.

Sheila pauses outside the kiosk. It has started snowing again, drifting a soft new layer over the compacted pavement. She swipes it away from her face and turns back to the block. The caretaker is at the entrance, scraping at the ice with a shovel.

'Not that this'll do any good.'

Sheila walks past, nodding politely.

'And you're all over-loading the heating system, I suppose you know that!' He turns to shout, his voice following her into the hall. Snow has drifted into the lift, propped open as usual, and the smell of wet, dirty carpeting follows her up the stairs. Sheila settles herself into the armchair and dozes, coming half-awake to hear the steady chatter of the radio announcing that an ambulance has overturned on the way to an accident, that more snow is forecast. Night returns early. Outside a gang has taken over the road, scurrying black figures against white. They are building something, packing snow into hard blocks, raising two twin towers that lean toward one another in the centre of the street.

In the early night of evening Sheila stands at the window, shifting slightly on her feet in unconscious accommodation to the wind that sways the block, shifting on its roots like a huge tree. She sees that, outside, it is a giant figure they are constructing, the twin towers its thick legs. She goes into the kitchen to survey her stockpile of tins, hoarded against famine or the crumbling of the city, or against the time when a remembered starvation will return. Not wanting to break into it, she makes a cup of tea. Perhaps it is the rocking of the building but she feels restless, on edge. The radio warns against exposing naked skin in the ambient temperature.

She puts on her winter work cap, winds a scarf around her mouth, and goes out, slamming the door to. The wind seems to drive down the corridors now, and up the stairwell.

The street is bathed in a particular yellow-blue light. The street lamps flicker uncertainly as the voltage wavers. Sheila detours around the main road, where the boys are gathered about their statue, torso-high now. The back streets are quiet with drifted snow, loud with the flinging of the wind against doors and windows.

No light shows at the front of the basement stairs, but the door opens to her knock. She steps inside and begins to unwind clothes from about her face.

'Plenty here tonight, considering.'

'Yeh? My hands are too cold to sign the damn book.'

She pushes past the curtain into the bar. There are a few at the tables, a few more lined up at the bar, a woman hunched over the jukebox. No one raises their eyes as she enters. Sheila slides her elbow onto the polished wood.

The barwoman lines up beer and chaser in front of her: 'A long way to come.'

'No distance too great.'

She turns to look around. The women sitting at the tables have a youthful look of triumph: as if they are here for the challenge of getting here alone, against a peculiar set of odds. They talk cheerfully amongst themselves of the snow, and whether it will be colder still on the way home.

'Well, and here you are, the old guard.' Bertha has moved along the bar towards her.

'Christ.'

'Not offended by that, are you?' Bertha places her red, swollen hand on Sheila's shoulder.

'Surprised you made it, Bertha.'

'Oh, I can still hobble.'

The woman at the jukebox punches buttons, sending a sudden wave of sound into the room. Sheila feels a presence behind her, Sunshine in a white dinner jacket, waiting.

'You going to buy me one or move, little white pig?'

Sheila looks up into her half-closed eyes, a good two feet above her: 'My mother was Armenian. Scotch?'

Someone turns up the volume on the jukebox. Sunshine settles her elbows on the bar, poking her long, white-clad legs into the room. The creases on her trousers stand up, sharp.

'How did you get that suit here in one piece?'

'You have to remember, the snow don't reach to my ankles.'

'You can carry me home.'

'I have other plans. Though I don't know, looking at this.'

Sunshine stares into the corners of the room.

'I can't stand the way these people look. Like little buns need to go in the oven.'

Sheila drains her glass and turns to nod at the woman behind the bar, 'I don't know why you're telling me this.'

'Oh, you,' Sunshine crosses her legs neatly, 'you look more like an old yellow tree root. Maybe it's that Armenian grandmother.'

'She'd like to hear that.'

Sunshine looks at her sidelong, 'Though you didn't dress to come out, did you. Letting the side down, Letiva. I have to achieve elegance all by myself?'

Bertha leans round in front of Sunshine, 'Dance with me, Sheila.'

They take small steps around the floor. Bertha leans

heavily, her hands grasping the supporting the body.

Sheila winces, transferring weight off her bad leg, 'This is the one-legged leading the crippled, you know.'

'So who else would bother?'

They sway gently from side to side, a motion as slight as the apartment block in the gale. Out of the corner of her eye Sheila watches Sunshine casually walk the perimeter of the dance floor. The place is filling, more late night adventurers, pioneering across the snow. They are banked up against the bar, laughing and blowing on their fingers. Bertha comes to rest against a stool and sinks onto it. At the card table someone deals Sunshine a hand. She sits, crumpling her legs around a chair.

'You can go away. I don't need minding.'

'I'm just resting.'

Sheila starts into another beer, watching the circling of the crowd. On the dance floor a group of them have formed into a circle. They swoop in and out, stamping their feet. They turn to face outwards, threatening to capture those drifting at the edges of the dance. Sheila turns her face carefully away from them. Her eyes flicker over the mirror tiling. Someone looks back at her, grinning, raising her eyebrows. Sheila glances along the bar: yellow hair, wide mouth. She stares back, begins to tunnel through the crush.

Close up her youth is too obvious, the glow of her skin frightening: 'Like to dance?'

'No.' Sheila looks into her beer, rolling down her shirt-sleeves against that gaze.

'Just to drink.'

'Yes.'

The child leans lightly on the bar next to her. Sheila tightens her grip on her glass.

'Muscular forearms.'

'Manual labour, that's what it does.'

She lays her arm along the counter beside Sheila's: 'Me too. Carpentry.'

Sheila examines the sinews laid out for her inspection, the long fair hairs shimmering under the lights: 'So I see.'

'I was going to say, did you want to spend an evening

with us girls playing poker,' Sunshine's hand tweaks her shoulder, 'but I see that you don't.'

'Another time.'

They walk down the middle of the road. The wind flattens snow against walls and fences. Down a side-street a fight is in progress; dozens on either side crouch behind barricades, hurling weighted snowballs. The wind carries their cries across the quiet city. The women glance as they pass and walk on. Sheila lengthens her stride.

The snow giant stands unfinished across the street, his waist reaching above their heads. They approach from behind; it could be the rough casting of the heroic worker, whose arms will be raised in a triumphal salute, whose eyes pierce the far horizon. They round the torso and look up: vast genitals hang over them.

'I don't like it.' She reaches down into the snow at her feet.

'Don't do that, much too obvious.' Sheila eyes it up and down, 'You want to go for the knee cap, very painful and makes him fall over.'

She takes aim and kicks out, driving her heel into the giant knee that looms at her chest. Her heel jars into the ice, a solid, impenetrable block. Pain spreads in flashes up her leg. She sits in the snow, bent over it.

'Are you all right?'

'Don't say anything, I don't want to hear it.'

She pushes herself to her feet and limps off down the street. The other follows at a slight distance.

'This is where I stop.'

'Shall I come up with you?'

Sheila looks carefully at her: 'All right. I don't feel so deathless tonight.'

They climb the stairs slowly, a step at a time.

'I could give you a piggyback.'

'No.'

'I'm not trying to make myself indispensable.'

'That would be stupid. Like kicking a block of solid ice.'

In the sudden heat of the flat the child divests herself of layers of clothing, revealing large bones.

Sheila is skilful, and prepared to concentrate for now, knowing that in the morning this person will drift off across the snow. Mona allows herself to be overtaken. If she feels a little invaded, held, her abandonment is deliberate and she finds a comfort in it.

Briefly they lie in silence, listening to the wind.

'Does it often rock like this?'

'You get used to it.'

Sheila reaches out and turns on the radio, 'I need to know if there are trains.'

They sleep disjointedly. The radio plays classical music and delivers unchanging bulletins on the state of the weather.

In the early dawn she is at the window, looking down. 'I like heights. You don't have to get up, I've been listening, there aren't any trains.'

'What's your name?'

'Mona.'

Wrapped in her coat, she stares out at a steady fall of snow. It is a long way to her room at the other side of the city, a longer journey than she wants to make. She puts on the kettle in the kitchen and spreads her hands over the glowing ring.

Sheila wakes again to tea, laid formally on a tray. The dried milk has been mixed to a thin liquid in a jug, Mona has arranged the biscuits on a plate.

'I can't drink tea like this, like a guest house.'

'It's tea in bed.'

'A block of ice, remember?'

Mona shrugs and lifts the teapot to pour.

Sheila clears the plate of crumbs with her finger: 'I think you should go now.'

'It's a long way across the city.'

Sheila leans back against the pillows and closes her eyes.

'Do you always do these things only once?'

She nods, 'It's safer, you'll find that out.'

'I don't want safety.'

Mona buttons her coat and leaves, stuffing a biscuit into her pocket. Sheila watches the dark, bundled figure walking quickly up the street, passing the great snow man without a glance.

She stands at the window. The snow sculpture is almost finished. A man standing on another's shoulders wields a knife, carving crisp pectoral muscles across his chest. Another stands below, shaping a calf. As Sheila watches they stand back, letting the blades dangle in their hands. The giant stands, casual and immense.

*

The woman in the cage looks reproachfully at her greasy, rumpled notes.

'Put me on the list, please. Letiva.'

'It's very busy.'

'Eight-thirty is all right.'

She writes, a scrawl in the empty space. When the time for her massage comes it will be slurred, garbled, an excuse to pass her over. Sheila takes a towel from the pile and pushes through the doors.

The heat is immediate and extraordinary. She leaves overalls, woollens, underwear in heaps like long-dead past skins to lie on the cubicle bed. Just to feel the strangeness of warm wet air on her skin.

In the steam room they sit vacantly, watching moisture condensing on the ceiling. Watery sweat pours down their bodies, soaking the slatted bench. Sheila sags forward, closing her eyes: there is no pleasure in this, merely the necessary, mechanistic opening of pores. She feels her hair flattening down, settling thickly onto her scalp.

They are lying in rows in the hot rooms, feet splayed, arms hanging limp. The heat smoothes out their faces as if strain has run off like liquid to take refuge in the flesh that creases their bodies. In the outer chamber they are turning the pages of magazines or absently fingering the skin of their upper arms. In the hottest chamber they are silent, still, only the eyelids flickering. There is no sound other than an occasional exhalation of breath, a sigh at the power of heat to prostrate them.

Sheila walks through the chambers, lifting her feet quickly from the hot stone floor. On a vacant bench in the hottest room she lies down and closes her eyes.

Lying thus, she is so well disguised. Flesh has collected in the same places, at the backs of the thighs, beneath the ribs, above the elbows. As she lies in the hot, dry room, sweat gathers in the same hollows. For a moment, her limbs relaxing against the slats, Sheila feels herself almost at one, merged with them in a common pursuit. And yet in in the centre of her there is something else that she knows they can see if they should look. As the woman at the entrance does, her eyes boring.

Slumped in the cooling room, she waits to catch her name, delivered mangled to the masseur. All around the walls they lean, limp exhausted bundles.

The masseur digs her fingers into knotted muscles, 'Manual labour.'

'Yes.'

'Like this – I've bands of steel in my back.'

Sheila wonders what kinship is intended.

'Ten hours a day I do this – worse than scrubbing floors.'

She runs her hands quickly up the thighs, diving suddenly with her thumbs.

'Felt that, I expect?' Sheila gasps.

'Funny thing, the body,' thumbs knead the soles of her feet. She strokes her soapy brush up and down the backs of the legs, 'When you know about the muscle structure, you can tell it's all a waste of time. But they will try to change themselves.' She sighs, rolling Sheila over onto her back with one hand.

Two of them are testing the plunge pool with their toes, a ritual dance. Small children at the edge of the ocean, they run back as soon as they feel that cold touch. Sheila stands beside them, looking into the blue water. They eddy backwards and forwards, laughing, hands over their mouths.

Sheila walks down the steps deliberately, walling herself against the icy water. Waist-deep, she swims a few strokes. As she climbs out they look her over, standing naked and quivering.

'Isn't it cold?'

'Of course, but exhilarating.' Heat pounds and darts across her skin.

They look at her blankly: 'Oh, it's too cold.'

'I don't know how you can.'

She shrugs: 'You make up your mind.'

They hitch their towels around them and look away from her, at their feet, the marbled ceiling, the play of bubbles on the blue water. Sheila climbs the stairs to her cubicle wearily, one foot dragged after the other. Found out in another bizarre distinction, the capacity to walk through iced water for the pleasure of getting out, warm, on the other side.

The tea comes in a tall glass, the fragment of lemon lurking at the bottom, suggesting repeated use. Sheila dips in her sugar cube and sucks. The woman in the booth raises her eyes at the sound. They look at one another, at old poverty showing: ah, but to have had your own sugar cube, all to yourself, then. Sheila grins and crunches noisily, throwing the sugar to the back of her mouth. In the booth the woman ducks her head, runs her finger down the massage list, mouthing words.

✷

She finds the kitten on the third floor landing, long-legged and greasy, black and some colour that might be white, pressed back into a corner. She leans her shoulder against the wall, waiting for the throbbing in her leg to ease. The cat watches her, its eyes wide. When she picks it up its body is cold in her hand. She shifts it under her elbow and continues her slow shuffling progress up the wall.

She takes out a bowl, mashes some water into dried milk. 'You realise this is a one night stand. I wouldn't want you to get hurt.'

When it has finished the bowl she puts down some more.

In the morning her head aches and the cat seems expectant. She looks down at it in the kitchen, 'I suppose I usually give them breakfast.'

It has drunk most of the milk. She makes them each a cup of weak tea. At the last moment she thinks to crumble a slice of bread into the cat's bowl.

She puts it on the third landing, leaving it abruptly as she turns from others before they can think of claiming continuity.

That evening, and for two days, the lift is on. Coming home on the third day, the door is lying propped open. Without seeming to look, Sheila turns to the stairs.

It is on the third landing. When she stands over it the eyes open. She picks it up; perhaps it is bound to die anyway. But dying, sometimes that changes the rules. She carries it up in her hand.

It eats bread and milk, 'Hedgehog food,' she says. Later, a tin of baked beans. It lies in front of the electric fire, distended. Sheila watches; it does not seem prepared to die.

ELSEWHERE: TWO

A enters her morning's results into the terminal. A day like any other, the usual record of this or that infringement. Only one that she cannot quite classify: sometimes motivation is so well concealed, it will take her finest skill to hunt it down. She goes back to the court report. A is relieved that there is no insanity plea; vague categories offend the subtleties of her system. She sees that no reasons of any kind have been put forward for his actions: violence out of a blue sky. A checks that she has not misplaced a page of the transcript, accustomed to mitigations. In the witness stand he is his own character reference, respectable, stolid, a pillar of the community.

A relinquishes her link with the computer. She rereads the details, seeking to infiltrate his mind. As the prosecutor sets the scene A imagines his voice, sonorous in the quiet room.

A rest-day morning, at the beginning of the year, and we have just come out of church. The minister has drawn a parallel, inspiring, between the regeneration of life in the spring and our human capacity for starting anew, shedding our sin like an outmoded garment. And there are indeed snowdrops beside the path that leads from the church door. We are a little troubled by indigestion, a common trouble in our later years, but there is a faint wintry sun and the prospect of a short nap before lunch. Things, on the whole, are as they should be.

And yet something attracts our attention to that woman, still sniffing, notoriously incapable of coming to church with a handkerchief. Her coat is too short at the back, it rides up over her arse. We have spent some time tidying the hymnals and come out behind her. She is almost the last out. Having no doubt remained on her knees making some ill-advised and importunate request. She is going in our direction, as you might expect, forcing us to look at her all the way down the road.

We might turn off here and go round the back to the tobacconist's. We're almost out. People keep their gardens very scruffy around this way, not much sign of spring regenerating here. And now look, there she is again, coming round the corner, you'd think she was pursuing us. We find it quite annoying.

It is here, the quiet of the street called up, the mild irritants particularised, that the prosecutor breaks away, launching suddenly into the details of the laurel bush beneath which they found her body, the torn and disarrayed state of her clothing. A flicks back through the pages: the motivation implied is that of the accused's distaste; the law's case is that he has taken a natural feeling much too far. An expert on the quantification of impulse, on the combinations of particular circumstances that may lead to a loss of self-control, A feels that any classification on this basis will be too superficial. She is, after all, concerned to achieve accuracy, to protect the integrity of her system.

At night she dreams atavistically of the man leaving the church, of the woman left gasping in the laurel bushes. Yet in the dawn she wakes alert, the solution clear in her mind. It is simple, it is of course fully documented, and only an aberration, perhaps some passing sickness, can have prevented her from seeing it before.

The office is still cool in the early morning, the air smells lightly of the cleaners' perfumed humidifiers. It is a matter of a moment to classify the attack: *misplaced violence, unattached object substituted*. She moves on, working quickly to make up for the time she has wasted. She ought to make a note of her mistake in her psychological profile; certainly she will do so if she has another lapse.

In the evening, she has half-an-hour to spare. Playfully she feeds the data of the man's case into the computer; who was it, she asks, that he really wanted to do that to? A few minutes later the computer comes back, chattily, *your guess is as good as mine*.

A looks at the screen and swears. After a moment she tries again, asking the question differently. The computer responds at once: *there is no evidence*, it says, *of anyone perpetrator wished, consciously or otherwise, to assault*.

Again A spends the night wrestling with her problem. Perhaps her programming is at fault – the computer does not always recognise motives when they are buried in a particular way within the data. A writes new formulae on the pad beside her bed, adding to her notes intermittently throughout the night. In the morning she rises sluggishly, half-dazed. But she has the outlines of a new programme, something at once sweeping in its scope, and detailed, a mesh through which no motive can hope to escape.

A begins to reprogramme. She slowly tests and retests, finding loopholes, removing inconsistencies. When it is finished, raw but complete in its structure, she again feeds in the report of the man who came out of church. She waits, quietly confident, while the computer sorts through the myriad complexities of her new system. She does not see the words appearing on the screen, but when she looks up they are there: *no motive discoverable.*

A goes home, despairing. At first she sleeps, heavily, for an unspecified time. When she wakes, it is to stare at the wall blankly, convinced of hopelessness. Her art, her work, depend on the capacity to classify. Brought up against the unclassifiable, the edifice crumbles. When A finally drags herself from bed, a mesh of assumptions confront her, newly questionable. It seems to her that her every act of classification must have been founded on the same error as that she has suddenly and so clearly discovered. She casts about for solidity, and finds an absence. She must have thought, a hundred, a thousand times, that a motive was clear, while all the time she had it wrong, had the wrong one, her psychological systems quite awry.

It is after perhaps a week of this that A goes out, down to the marketplace to buy food. She is light-headed for lack of it, her feet seeming hardly to touch the ground, but the objects around her appear clearer, brighter, their edges sharply delineated. It is in this condition that A sees in front of her a pile of oranges, a great heap, all jumbled together. Holding a bag in one hand, she reaches forward with the other to take one. As she does so she realises how they are similar, how random her choice will be. Her hand wavers, arrested over the pile.

A carries home with her a sense of revelation, feeling it to be precious and important without any clarity as to what it might be that she has perceived. At home, putting the oranges in a bowl and picking up her pad, she puts it all down as she has been taught, step by step.

There is, it is suddenly clear to her, no difference between one motive and the next. They are all equally applicable, equally inapplicable. Each time she has done a classification it has been as if she were picking an orange from the pile, a random process guided by her eye, her mood, the weather. A pauses, turning an orange between her fingers: he killed his mother because she was cruel to him, he killed his mother because someone had dropped a brick on his foot that day at work – it made no difference, it was not an illumination. A digs her nails into the pith of the orange, exhilarated. What mattered, she sees at last, was the act itself. Did he kill his mother? He did.

A lies awake at night, light-headed still, but buoyed up now by the speed at which her mind is working, sifting the significances of her discovery. Again she reviews the years past: years spent in the pursuit of a chimera. A sees this and shrugs it off, a necessary prelude perhaps, but at any rate now an irrelevance. Her mind speeds on to consider the future. In her head she outlines a new programme, simple now that there is no need for complex, obfuscatory classifications.

The next morning she is so early arriving that she meets a cleaner on the way out. They look one another up and down carefully. A smiles but the cleaner only grimaces. A shrugs as she sits down over the terminal. One day, perhaps, she will understand.

A labours through the day to retrieve information and to sort it. Some of what she had classified long ago is reluctant to emerge, well-hidden within the neat confines of her carefully nurtured system. Some of what she finds has become meaningless, some vital connecting thread lost in the process of storage. A nods to herself, passing on; it only confirms her analysis of what has gone before.

By evening she has moulded the data to her needs. At

her fingertips, now, she has the details of a thousand acts of violence, the details of their perpetrators, their lives, the means of finding them. A sits in the dusk, her face lit by a faint radiance from the empty screen, and considers her creation. She finds it pleasing.

A takes another day off from her office and walks towards the nearby hills. She searches for a purpose for the weapon she has created from the long unused, sleeping data. She feels sure that the proper use for her hoarded information will emerge in front of her, clear as the pile of oranges.

She walks up a steep track between mounds of sharp rocks. Below her the valley waves with bracken. The path twists as it rises; sometimes she catches a glimpse of the other side of the mountain and the valley beyond. A climbs, her mind occupied with the business of ascending, of placing her feet carefully on the sharp scree. At the summit there is a wide flat stone. Lying down on it, A does not feel the wind, only the warm sun shining down clear. A rests for a while. When she sits up there is an old man coming towards her up the other side of the mountain. He is carrying a stick and an old brown haversack. A is embarrassed by her new blue walking shoes. The old man reaches the rock and sits down suddenly; A can hear the breath rasping in his chest. They sit in silence staring out over the landscape, and A realises that she has spoken to no one for a long time.

The old man takes a thermos flask out of his bag and gingerly unscrews the lid. A watches as he arranges two cups and a twist of sugar on the flat stone in front of him. From another pocket of the bag he brings out a paper bag containing biscuits. He looks up at her watching, and smiles. I generally find someone up here to take tea with, he says, I'm afraid there's no lemon. But I prefer milk, A says hurriedly, immeasurably hungry.

They drink and eat biscuits, scattering crumbs across the stone and the grass. A puts two lumps of sugar in her tea, though she would normally drink it without. It is very peaceful here, A says, feeling that she is saying something important. The old man is silent for a time. Perhaps, he says at last, it is because the violent do not climb so high. A feels cold, remembering the problem she has left behind. If only I could stay here, away from them, she says. And what would the rest of the world do, the old man asks, not every peaceful person can perch on top of a mountain. He begins to gather together the cups and to sweep crumbs off the stone into the grass. Then he lifts his hand and disappears down the side of the mountain. After a while, A notices his stick, still propped against the stone. She runs to the edge with it, waving. At a great distance already, he shakes his head. I don't need it, now that I'm going down, he calls thinly, keep it.

A goes down the mountain, the stick swinging in her hand. Down in the valley she twirls it above her head like a baton, so fast that it blurs through the air. As she reaches the town she waves it in front of her, the slicing weapon of a martial artist.

She goes directly to her office, carrying the stick discreetly through quiet evening corridors, past silent screens and chairs. The terminal sighs into life under her hands. A begins to print out lists, long detailed and precise: the perpetrators of violence described, pinpointed. A then returns to another list, the list that in her mind she thinks of as the interested parties. Those on the second list, they will know what to do with the information on the first. Given this weapon, they will take action into their own hands. Soon A has a pile of envelopes beside her, neatly addressed to subversive places. A feeds the pile through the mailing system; it seems to her appropriate to continue to use official channels. She is doing no more than what is necessary to bring the fruits of her research to bear upon her data.

Later, in her room, A sits and looks at the stick she has been given, passing it from hand to hand. It occurs to her that she may have misinterpreted the message she took the stick to contain. But that is the chance that any cryptic seer must have to put up with. A feels that it is no concern of hers. She sleeps soundly.

Her position gives A ample opportunity to observe the results of her dissemination of information. There is soon a quite notable variation in the statistics that arrive daily at her office for tabulation. In the months following her action, there is a sudden rise in the numbers of crimes of violence for which no perpetrator can be traced. This trend proves vexatious to the analysts, as it renders assessment of motive more difficult, even hazardous. A plays her part cheerfully in the resolution of this problem, meanwhile checking the identity of the victims against those in her first list. She finds that within three months five per cent of those identified have been targeted. Although she experiments with several classification modes she cannot discover any pattern to those who have been chosen. A is at first irritated by this and expends considerable energy in the search. Eventually, however, she realises that it is in the nature of those on the second list that they should deliberately be using a means of selection that will not be accessible to her methods of analysis. She finds that she sometimes remembers dreams that suggest possible methods: pieces of paper being crumpled into a hat; a child playing a skipping game, chanting names as she jumps the rope.

STREET SCENE: TWO

They are spread about the living room, jackets strange in the indoor light.

Liz sits – only waiting to be out of there, mind flexing for the door. She cannot remember how she could have come. She does not want to risk herself on the streets anymore, it is hard enough just staying alive. The baby weighs her down. She looks only at Gloria, who will surely understand. That not everyone has her own unnatural strength.

Tam twitches, interlacing her fingers. She trusts no one, there is something too easy about them all. She sees them all sliding into their niches: Liz is no surprise. In the street she would cross the road when she saw Tam coming. Tam is defending herself and Liz already has too many protectors.

Looking round, Sue sees herself marked off, the next to go. She searches for words to cloak the naked proof of her need to prowl the exciting dark. Lust is not a reason she can advance.

Gloria leans heavily into her chair. All she needs just now is sleep. Would give her soul for it, were anyone offering. She notices that they are none of them noticing that. Too used to her pushing aside everything to see the will behind it anymore, the great drain of that striving. She wonders if it is her own blooming for which she is turning over this hard ground.

Ruth and Sheila exchange glances: it is as they expect. Loyalty that is given as a matter of choice will not bear them up, it has no substance. But Sheila does not hold the look; it is too long since she aquired resignation. Ruth desires the simple purity of a betrayal and yet she is tied, feeling Liz's departure somehow her responsibility. She has failed to woo the diffident recruit: another lost to the sweeter scent of talcum powder.

Layers of time, days and decades, pile their wafer sheets in Elsie's head. These women so conscious of being different, disparate, merge into so many other occasions, so many similar acts of balance.

'I don't have the time.' Liz inspects the floor. How the dust has built up.

'You think I do?' Gloria only lifts a weary hand, the slightest movement.

Ruth grins: 'Some of us are dispensable.'

'I'm not going to anymore. You think this is the only thing that has any meaning?'

'You have your reasons.' Sheila has learnt to absorb the inevitable, daily as breakfast.

Ruth gets to her feet: 'Going to take one more night's risks?'

'Of course.'

'Oh, attagirl.' Tam clenches her hand around the door handle as if it were the neck of a bird.

Elsie watches them out the door: they seem to stumble and lurch tonight, as if the rage and anger had collected in their knees. They are shabby and pathetic, surely, inadequate instruments of her delicate schemes. Incompetent to their own designs, even, their own personal acts of vengeance.

It has begun to rain. They walk with their heads down.

'You didn't tell me.'

Liz hunches her shoulders, 'D'you think I would? We don't speak to one another.' She walks faster, 'And don't say, we're partners.'

'I wouldn't say that.'

'Do you think I haven't needed help?'

'No.'

Liz stops under a projecting shopfront. 'Let's stop here.'

Let them come to us, if they're going to.'

'They're more likely, to go somewhere else.'

'So, we aren't guarding the whole world.'

'Nothing doing tonight.'

Gloria jerks her head at the lighted windows. 'Makes you wonder what they're doing inside.'

Tam knows minutely, the landscape of her experience.

'She's just sitting there hoping the tv don't fall apart. Or some kid finally got rid of her damn brother so she can do it on the settee. Cushions all bunched up.' Her voice is high and flattened: 'And maybe the baby screaming, and you yelling shut up. And your grandma coming in in the middle, ah Tammy, I thought you called.'

She sucks in a breath and they laugh, and forget to notice the man in the telephone box, not dialling a number. Under the lamp-post, as they pass, the light shines on rain resting in Gloria's hair.

'This is what I would expect of you, Tammy, that's what she said.'

Tam's litany falters and Gloria takes her within her arm so that they walk close, 'She's white, your grandma?'

Down the street the kiosk door thuds gently. He puts his rolled newspaper under his arm.

'They all are, aren't they, except him.'

They walk, long paces over the glistening pavements. In the silence, Gloria waits.

'He went back, you know. Why didn't he take me?'

She laughs. They stop under a tree. Gloria grips the railings, Tam leans her head against the bark.

The man pauses, seeing them stopped. He cannot see what they are doing, for the rain. Abruptly, tiring of the silence, he turns away. Let them stand in the rain; it is nothing to him.

'When you're ready,' Gloria says, coming alert to the night.

In the small dryness under the awning, Liz smokes. Ruth leans against the plate glass, hands thrust into her armpits.

Liz shivers, 'I don't know what I'm waiting for.'

Ruth watches the pool in the gutter seeping outwards, across the road, 'For this to be over.'

'I think I'll go home.' To stay and get wet; that would be an empty gesture.

'Why don't you. No point getting wetter than you need, is there.'

'You'll go back, then?'

'Might wait for the rain to ease.'

Liz turns away toward the main road. The cabs would still be out, little yellow lights in the dark.

'She went home early.'

They giggle.

'She didn't ask you to escort her to the bus?'

'You shouldn't've stayed out after she went.'

Tam picks at the table with her fingernail, 'We'll have to find someone else.'

'Another nice girl for Ruth.'

'She likes them tall and Anglo-Saxon.' Gloria sprawls across the kitchen bench.

Tam looks up: 'We wouldn't know where to look, then.'

Elsie leans over, plunging a plate of biscuits onto the table, pushing aside the temporary insanity of the night, the strangeness that they bring back in with them. Would tear anything to shreds now, hounds with the blood up.

Tam draws the plate toward her: 'You come out with us, Elsie.'

'Not my kind of thing.'

'Women shouldn't be reckless, after all.'

Tam laughs, 'Who told you that, Sheila?'

'Some long dead little bird.'

Elsie stands by the table: 'It's four o'clock in the morning.'

SOURCE MATERIAL: ELSIE

The chair squeaks as she swivels to and fro, lulling herself into a trance in the tenth-floor window. The early winter dark hangs, about to fall. Elsie keeps her eyes averted from the shimmering nylon knees placed confidentially close to her chest. But Rose goes on sitting on the desk, facing her, her mouth goes on opening and closing.

'Tell them they'll miss the money.'

Rose make a small gesture, lifting her hands. 'They say I'm never there. They don't eat properly.'

Elsie is conscious overwhelmingly of her reticence. The layers of silence are so many that she has almost lost any sense of saying anything. Looking at Rose, the list of that which she may not say rises in front of her. If she were to open her mouth too suddenly or too wide it seems it might all spill out: don't you know you're surrounded, don't you see it killing you? Haven't you noticed the prices rising and the jobs getting fewer, the uniforms merging into one mass and the people looking through your letterbox? Can't you see that you're helpless, and always will be, while alone?

'Maybe your father-in-law should learn to cook, since he's at home all day.'

Rose rocks back on the desk, laughter spilling in little gushes from the side of her mouth. She rocks and rocks, holding her stomach, her knees seesawing, 'I'd like to see him wearing an apron.'

Elsie wonders who Rose thinks she is speaking to, this person whose advice she seeks out but never takes. How ever little she may say, they go on coming to her with their complaints. Elsie will understand any injustice, never let you down. Rose is gathering herself together, smoothing down her skirt, forming her face into the right lines. She is going back to her typewriter unburdened, cleansed.

Elsie replaces the earphones and pushes the cassette home. The voice in her ears clears its throat and begins to dictate. She stares at the keyboard and dismembers the message carefully into single disconnected words.

*

There is a low mist on the fell across the valley. It hangs quiet, rising and falling slightly as if breathing, its scraggy lower edges mingling with the tips of the conifers.

'It will clear,' Marion says, 'no trouble at all.' She bites into her toast with emphasis.

She leads the way beside the river, the path squirelling round the bank, between thin birch trunks. Elsie walks cautiously, each step deliberate on the friable earth. They cross at the stepping-stones, Marion stopping midstream to stare downriver where the bed narrows and the water runs white.

'I do this walk every time I come, 'she says, 'and it never fails.'

'Never fails?'

'To uplift the spirit.' She turns and leaps to the further bank, her steps glancing and goat-like.

They stop on a higher level, where beech trees thin into pines. Marion divides cheese sandwiches with concentration. Elsie, watching, is reminded of a past dedication to the cause.

'How's teaching?'

Marion does not look up from her task: 'Predictable. But anything would be by now, wouldn't it.'

'It didn't turn out to be your life's work.'

'I've spent my life doing it, that's enough.'

Elsie lowers the sandwich from her mouth, 'Is it?'

'We learn to look elsewhere, don't we.' Marion peels an orange precisely, 'I shall move up here, eventually.'

'To live?'

'It can be done, you know. I like it here.'

Elsie looks into the layered branches, 'I can't imagine leaving the city.'

They shake pine needles out of the folds of their trousers. Marion shoulders the haversack and turns upwards, on through the trees.

They climb a stile and are suddenly beyond the forest, bare fell in front of them.

Marion points upward, 'The mist has lifted, after all. There'll be a view.'

'How d'you know when you reach the top?'

'There's a pile of stones. And you can't go any higher.'

Above them the wind flattens the grass. Marion stands looking ahead, her hair pushed out in front of her, poised for the summit. Elsie swings her other leg over the stile.

The wind gusts, making them sway on their feet.

'You could fall off here, 'Elsie says, putting her back against the bedraggled heap of stones.

'I can make out the northern fells.' Marion takes a chocolate bar out of her pocket. They eat in silence, staring out across the grey-white valley to mist-blurred hills.

'What is it keeps you in the city, Elsie?'

'Other than my job, or being tired?'

'You make it sound as if there was more.'

Elsie draws her eyes from the emptiness of the sky. 'You would find it hard to understand.'

'I still live there,' Marion divides the last square of chocolate between them.

'Yes.'

They follow a sheep path, twisting down the fellside. Elsie feels the fragility of her ankles as Marion jumps lightly between tussocks. On the broad smooth track below Marion waits expectantly. Elsie gathers herself, walking beside her.

'I organise a small vigilante group.'

Their feet crunch loudly in the stillness; the wind has dropped. 'Just a few women spending their Saturday nights prowling around, looking for street violence. Liberal, I know, only a subversive gesture.'

'Not liberal –'

'There's no structure, an individual thing, can have no ultimate significance. Anarchic foolishness.' She wishes to explain, that she too has lost faith.

'And how do you justify this?'

Elsie waves an arm at the landscape, 'Justify. . . I'm not an idealist any more, Marion. I will use any means to achieve something. I don't worry about justifying myself.'

'I can't see what you do hope to achieve.' Marion's pace has quickened, her legs reaching out eagerly to cover the ground.

'No, I don't suppose you do. I've been reduced to stirring up trouble, Marion. Who can predict anymore, what the spark will be that lights the fire?'

Marion manages almost to smile: 'I thought we didn't believe in random sparks.'

They are back in the darkening quiet of the pine wood, their striding, headlong pace slowed by the sliding layer of needles beneath their feet.

'Women? What sort of women are they?'

Elsie grimaces: 'A funny lot, really. Just like any other –'

'Most women don't roam the streets looking for trouble.'

'No,' Elsie says slowly, 'but there's nothing special about these because they do, exactly.'

'It makes no sense. What good does it do?'

'Sense? No, it makes no sense that they're desperate enough to go out and do something futile and dangerous. But perhaps they don't see it like that. I can't provide sense, Marion, that's the last thing in the world I can give you.'

'The way down is shorter. Soon be back to the river.' Marion lightens her voice, eagerly, 'Still a passionate espouser of causes, I see.'

Elsie shrugs: 'I don't really think I have any passion left.'

'What then?'

'I must make use of what there is to hand.'

The path takes them down steadily, to the river. They pause on the bridge to watch the slow flow of water, the river spreading across the valley floor.

'The house is in front of us, we've come almost full circle.'

Elsie looks at the water: 'Explanations aren't important. Understanding is not what matters any more.'

Elsie stands under the white glare of the supermarket lights turning vegetables in her hands. The lights seem too bright, as if there were really something to conceal here. She glances round. It is a mentality, once gained, that you never lose: the instinct for those watching you, the need to hide, the signs of conspiracy. The violent lights and these gigantic bins of produce, they are to tell us that we live in a sunny, abundant world. Elsie lifts a bag into her basket and turns away, tired of these perceptions that illuminate nothing, since no one is listening.

She turns the pages of the scrapbook: Elsie and Ben in Yugoslavia, '59. Delegation, October '60. A huddle of sheepskin coats, that conference on the coast, sea in the background. Elsie peers at the picture more closely, is that him, smiling in the second row? Terence Thomas, the life and soul of the meeting. Charm, and thick black hair, and large warm hands. Elsie lowers the book to the table: fundamentally unserious, Terry was always that. Extraordinary that they'd put up with him at all. Made out that selling papers on corners gave him the chance to accost all the pretty girls. Ben used to say he said that to annoy, that underneath he was a true zealot. They always were allies of a sort, those two.

She makes herself walk slowly to the door. 'Well, Terry, and after all these years.'

'Better late than never.' He reaches his arms around her in the darkness of the hallway.

He has brought a bottle of whisky. Elsie itemises proofs of prosperity as he hitches up sumptuous trousers and rests his polished shoes on the table. His eyes fall on the scrapbook and he smiles.

She puts out two glasses: 'It is a long time, isn't it.' And he looks as if the years have fulfilled his expectations.

'Not married again?' He is pouring doubles with a steady, practised hand.

'After Ben? No, no particular desire to, really.' Looking at him, Elsie can quite well guess that he is married now, to someone faithful and uncomplaining, of course. And that it will not have stopped him doing as he pleases.

He considers her, head on one side: 'You always were selfcontained, even then.'

'Was I?' Elsie thinks of herself as painfully open, then. Or else how had Terry got under her guard so easily?

'I never felt that I quite knew the real you, Elsie. Elusive.' Terry spreads his well-suited arm along the settee.

'Did you want to?' As Elsie remembers, he had just wanted her to capitulate, prove he could take her away from Ben. . . . Even her, the group's most rigorous moralist. Sod the real person, it was the power he wanted.

'You wouldn't've known what to do with the real me, Terry. She might've got in your way.'

He holds his glass critically to the light: 'Ever hear from Ben at all?'

'Sends me a birthday card sometimes.'

'That was a great waste, you know, you two not getting back together.'

Elsie pours herself another drink, lining bottle and glasses up neatly on the table, 'So now you're feeling nostalgic about a marriage you broke up?'

'I didn't break it up, you know. You did.' Terry smiles, as if lightly sugaring a necessary pill.

'I suppose you don't see him either?'

Terry waves a hand in the direction of his elegantly-shod feet, 'I've lost contact with that crowd since I set up on my own. Success doesn't go with socialist principles, does it.'

'And what brings you here to see me?'

Terry watches her swallow her drink at a gulp: 'I don't think you're appreciating that fine malt.'

'We failures can't afford to acquire the taste.'

‘Thought I’d like to see how you’d got on. One retains an interest in some things, some people, don’t you think.’

‘Sexually, do you mean?’ Elsie sinks back into her chair. Age seems to have affected his power to charm. Though probably not his capacity to secure what he wants.

‘No one’s ever managed to teach you to be less blunt, have they?’ Unhurriedly Terry refills her glass.

He is still strong, muscular as if he works out in a gym after his business lunches. He lifts her easily, despite the extra weight that has gathered about her since the last time he tried anything similar. Perhaps he has noticed the narrow bed next door, the uninviting chill in the air, for he only carries her as far as the sofa that he has sprawled across all evening. The cushions under her still hold his warmth. He is polite and smooth, holding his weight off her carefully, not fumbling at any catches. He undresses her the minimum amount and Elsie understands that this is an attempt at tact, that they should not confuse the present activity with romantic passion or the excesses of youth. On the whole it reminds her of adolescence, a much more polite and civilised version of that cold and partial exploration in the backs of vehicles. It has the same anatomical flavour, as of a controlled experiment. She feels a mild but distinct sense of achievement when the experiment is successful, as if she has found she can still ride a bicycle after a long absence.

For a moment he rests, leaning his head on her shoulder. Then his hand reaches out to their half-full glasses: ‘Aren’t you glad I called round?’

Elsie watches his wide hands cradling the glass: ‘Up on a business trip?’

‘Just for the day. Must start the drive home soon.’

She sits at one end of the settee, pressing damp knees together. The last time this happened, she remembers now, it was in a hotel room in the middle of the afternoon when they should both have been at a session of the conference. Someone was reading an important paper and as a delegate she would be expected to report back to her group. But they were together that afternoon and he had given her beer, it was the middle of August, and because it was so hot he had made her lie on the floor by the window. They could hear the people on the seafront, and the sound of pebbles being dragged down the beach by the sea. All her meetings with Terry had that same raffish excitement, like escaping from the real world into a fairground. Terry was capitalist decadence, always, dealing with your sorrows by drowning them, one way or another.

'I'll make some coffee, then.'

She makes the coffee meticulously, warming the pot, adding an extra spoonful of grounds as this is company. He will be offended by the absence of a milk jug, she realises, and searches the back of the cupboard.

He is not in the front room when she comes back with the tray, has used the bathroom but is no longer in it. The only remains of his presence are the half-empty bottle, the rimed glasses and the scrumpled cushions on the settee. Elsie puts the tray on the table beside the glasses. It is not what she would expect of Terry, to whom appearances were always so important. Perhaps tomorrow he will send her flowers to cover his error. She pours herself a cup of coffee, against the feeling of loss clutching her sharp as cramp, against the vividness of the memory of his hands.

✵

Her mind weaves and turns at a little distance from the body sweating on the bed below.

'Finch,' she mutters automatically, seeing the bouncing flight across her window. The capacity to identify birds, another redundant skill from an era of a expectation. Innocence of youth, when outdoor activity of a studious and non-violent kind was healthy, and health so important for those with a future. What the vanguard might do on a Sunday for relaxation, political commitments permitting. Out to the gravel pits by motor-cycle for autumn-migrating waders. What health they had, and how easy it seemed to maintain it: take a breath of country air and forget your troubles. Forget your troubles? Extraordinary that that could have been believable, even then.

Elsie turns her head slightly on the pillow. There might well be places where the trees are not pock-marked and the cliffs are still full of ravens, but it makes no difference, now, to the flawed nature of the whole. It is unimaginable, almost, that there might have been a time when she had not known this.

She notes that the second hand of the clock has stopped, or is only moving very slowly, too slowly, too slowly for the naked eye to catch. But she is also aware that this is how the 'flu takes her, that she has only to lie quietly, charting the progress of the disease and taking the usual amount of pills. She turns away from the clock and stares instead at the electric fire, lying cold and inert on the mat. It is certainly beyond her strength, just now, to get out of bed and turn it on. She allows her eyes to close.

She wakes humming a little tune, the words to which remain elusive. The room seems colder. With resolution, Elsie places her legs on the floor and launches herself towards the wall and the fire. She reaches the switch and leans briefly, a leaf-like trembling at her knees. But the shuffle of her feet on the mat as she eases her way back to bed nudges at her memory, fitting words to the spritely tune.

> we don't get *ill*
> in the land arm-*ee*
> oh we don't get *ill*
> in the land arm-*ee*
> *do* we now, girls!

Sung to dry, stubborn cows and hay bales too heavy to lift, and plodding home across the fields exhausted. Wise-cracking city girls become grim and drawn, silenced by physical labour. That little song the tattered remnant of their ironical, fast moving former selves.

Shocked at first by the brutish simplicity, draining cows of milk, of calves, finally of meat, their bodies shoved, impregnated, kicked, transported, sliced. Used to find themselves, at first, too powerfully aware of some link between themselves and the lumbering beasts, might say into the night silence, 'I could've been born a cow, you know?' Soon became accustomed, impassive, as merely enduring as the herd itself. Would more likely lie briefly awake asking, 'Would you sell yourself for a hot bath?' Of course, they would say, easier as the months went by, there being so little hope for anything beyond a little comfort. Elsie draws her knees up to her chest, colder at the thought of that bleak, desolate empty country where the mind slept and faith was lost for lack of energy to sustain it.

You should never have gone. A reactionary search for agrarian bliss which you know is not the way of the future, they said. And back in the city she sold papers and shouted on street corners, swayed in packed meetings and saw hope re-emerge, as if an old grey leathery skin had been shucked off. Elsie winds her feet further into the blankets in search of warmth; the mistakes of youth are various, hope and despair. The electric fire has reddened into life and sits across the room humming and chattering, spitting out fragments of dust.

She wakes again in the afternoon darkness, her mouth dry. The water in the jug beside her is tepid. Time seems slow and inimical: years of this to come, lying in bed not quite warm, waiting for the dark; entertaining herself with scenes from the past and hoping for the strength to get to the toilet.

The clock hovers before three o'clock. It is the morning of the third day. Tomorrow it will begin to recede and you will be yourself again. Unfevered and competent, you will no longer want to be looked after in some alpine sanatorium, high and clear in the mountains. Above the noise of population, industry, struggle: where your only purpose is to rest, to get better, your only moral obligation to make the best use of the facilities at your disposal. You really ought to be soaking those aching muscles in an aromatic bath, Mrs Steiner. The blue sky, the black trees outside the window. Still sunlit rooms. Later, as strength returns, walking across crisp tight-packed snow, a small group walking unhurriedly, taking a simple pleasure in their regained mobility. Gradual relaxation, as the need to worry about the ailing body fades and the possibility of attention to others takes shape among them. Long evenings of disputation, then, the topics of irrepressible importance to them all. A meeting of eager minds, as eager as in the beginning. And the reawakening continues, body following the mind into the open. Nothing need be impossible or clouded in the clear, thin mountain air. Elsie sleeps fitfully, her arms crossed over her chest.

Outside in the garden a blackbird gives its alarm call, over and over. The winter branches give it no cover from the cat who crouches beneath. The bird looks and calls, arrested by the unwinking, stony stare. On the other side of the window Elsie tosses in her bed as the chattering call seeps into her dreams. It is early, hardly light. She opens her eyes with reluctance. The bird is only a few feet away; she can see its beak opening in repeated frenzy. It seems to Elsie, waking, that the vague dawn terrors of the city have found a voice and are broadcasting a warning, over and over.

The toast is cold and sodden by now but she pushes it into her mouth and chews slowly. With the same determination, she pours the last of the tea and adds a large amount of milk. Only when she has eaten and drunk everything does Elsie allow herself to lean back and close her eyes. It is the third day, appointed for the reassertion of normality. The first meal has been duly accomplished. It is natural, this retreat from reality in weakness, it is not to be taken any more seriously than that. The body is a reluctant instrument at times, would like to be able to take things easy. It likes to believe it is possible to evade suffering. Any fantasy will do. Time now to shake off that layer, sitting across her mind like an obsolescent film-script, and plunge back into the world. She is not going to indulge in a spiritual crisis, lie in bed and wonder what to do with her life. That is an activity for the uncertain, those who cannot accept a hard, continuing way. Illness, the fading or return of strength in her body, make no difference to the truth, or her choices. She will go on, using the corrupt, pathetic means at her disposal because nothing else is possible.

ELSEWHERE: THREE

. . .fragment remains on file, peripheral interest. . .

Subject identified according to description. She's fat, isn't she. I wasn't expecting that. Racial characteristic? To be honest I don't remember, get confused between the africans and these, I expect you know how it is.

Subject was wearing black leather jacket, a swirly skirt and a red handkerchief round her head. That was something to be following, it almost made it too easy. But these details, they have to be significant. Women don't dress like that for no reason. Walking behind her I got this strong hostile feeling. (You were clear about how we should not be afraid to be individuals, how that was the way the best information came over. Like the accidental scum on top of the dirty bath water that told you where your body had been, you said.) From the way she was walking, subject was not intending to go shopping. She was going down the road more like she owned everything and wasn't too concerned about how it was doing. That fits with how these people see life. Either they skulk about, convinced everybody's after them and the noose is inches from their neck, or they think they really have the answer and any minute now the world's going to fall into their lap. Subject looked like that, like she thought she had it all sorted out. I felt that it was a good thing I happened to be following her. (I realise on reflection that this can't have been coincidence, you must have assigned me, of course, and I hope I have lived up to your expectations.)

Subject walked for some twenty minutes through town in a north-westerly direction. I have checked the timetable and can confirm that she could nave taken a bus to her eventual destination. The walk will have been to avoid recognition on the transport system. Too many of them seem to know about the cameras. (I would like to suggest that lens surveillance be extended to street coverage in certain areas. Blanket vigilance is in my opinion the answer to our containment problem.)

Subject paused twice during route when accosted by others. First meeting was with man, also black, conventional appearance. Subject seemed not to be giving him her full attention, eager to be on her way. This suggested to me she must be going somewhere important; it isn't like them to pass up an encounter. On second occasion, subject came across a woman. White, flashy blonde hair, wearing a turquoise fake flying suit. The kind they make for women who are rich enough to find manual labour romantic. She looked like she thought she had the common touch. I was able to position myself within earshot of part of their conversation, during which subject was talking about baby-sitting. White woman seemed to be offering her services. I speculate that this conversation would have been about other activities, and would like to suggest a further investigation. I was quite clear that there were things going on beneath the surface between these two. It was the first time that I had encountered the desire for personal intervention. I had been expecting it, but the strength of it took me by surprise. . . I felt a real need to step right in there and interrogate at source. Hope that it might be possible to arrange this at a later date. (You said that it was important that we think in terms of getting satisfaction from our work. This means results, you said, and sometimes that means getting your hands dirty. I am fully prepared to do what is necessary.)

On arriving at destination, subject rang the doorbell. To think that these people imagine they can take over the world, and the best they can do for a signal is three squirts on the bell. But I shouldn't complain about what makes things a whole lot easier for me.

Subject remained inside for two hours. Without the equipment, of course, I cannot say what passed between them. But I took the opportunity to investigate the surrounding area. and was able to observe the subject for a large part of her stay through a ground floor window.

House in question is divided. Subject visited woman on ground floor. They sat in the kitchen, which looks out over the mess of dirty bushes and trees that passes amongst this crowd for a garden. Subject appeared to drink several cups of coffee and to eat slices of bread spread with something that came out of an unidentifiable plastic container. There was no sign of drug abuse, I think because these ladies take themselves too seriously, which is pretty laughable in itself.

Woman living in flat is white, small and lumpy. Looks like she gave up on herself about thirty years ago. Grey hair that hasn't seen the hairdresser for at least that long, she probably cuts it herself with the kitchen scissors. Wearing shapeless, bright-coloured trousers and some sort of sloganised tee shirt. Not the kind you'd bother to go with if she was lying in the gutter waiting for it.

A: Shall we allow this to continue? You can see how it has affected him. Quite instructive of the fragility of civilisation. Fortunate for our purposes that it is so superficial, I suppose.

B: One of those charming little paradoxes. But I never pretended to believe in the human race. Let the tape run a little, why don't you? He's just beginning to get going.

. . .it was almost dark, and her skirt swirled up the street. Walking like if she was in any doubt before, the dumpy one had just made it for certain, she was in line for queen the day after the revolution. I trailed subject all the way across town, I could see her fat arse all the way. . .

A: I really don't think this is going to turn out very original.
B: My dear, be patient.
A: We ought simply to erase.
B: Don't you want to know what he's done?

. . .it was pitch dark in there, and the walls had things

hanging on them. The corridor appeared to have been arranged to make a surprise entry difficult, as there was no clear path from the front door through the bedroom where the subject and her husband slept. I located. . .

B: He's got into the house – that's really quite impressive.
A: We should stop sending these people out.
B: They do get so involved, don't they.

. . .The son sleeps in a separate room. I thought about if it was a good idea to do him, as you had pointed out that it was a good idea if you could put the subject under stress without them knowing that it came from us. . .

A: He thinks he's in the execution squad now.
B: I told you he was going to be extravagant.
A: It's not that I mind the irresponsibility. But I'm not sure that this serves any purpose.
B: God moves in mysterious ways, my dear.

. . .brought these out with me. (These items are tagged and numbered. I was unable to discover the purpose of all items as this was my first contact with this kind of people.)

A: Well?
B: Oh, he may be right. These fanatics sometimes have a sixth sense for the worm that's about to turn.

SOURCE MATERIAL: RUTH

Ruth walks round the small rectangle of garden, pacing. From the far corner and the compost heap, to the almond tree, along the herbaceous border, past the kitchen window to the magnolia. Pause under the magnolia to look up into the branches, at the closed buds. She turns her back on their reluctance. Down to the compost heap again, along the narrow crazy paving slick with moss. That would have him out with the spray-can, fighting it back. Ruth looks down, she likes moss, has argued for its preservation for years. But now her feet slip on the path. By the almond tree she stops. The tree looks back at her, promising to blossom soon. It is only a short time to wait. It requires that she avert her eyes politely from the mess of ageing nuts lying unpicked at its feet. She moves on, striking out across the lawn. Pause for a last time, to look at the house. It seems the same. The bricks are the same dark red, the gutters are still black, the tiles of the roof lie symmetrically side by side.

'Ruthie.' She is at the bottom of the stairs, 'I don't know what he wants. He doesn't make any sense.'

Ruth nods and squeezes past. When she looks back, at the turn of the stairs, Sadie is sitting on the hall chair looking at the wall.

'Hello.'

He looks at her, 'Perhaps you can – the door. The door – open it, will you?'

The door is open. She gets up, closes it, opens it: 'Is that better?'

'Open it, please.' He is trying to be patient and rational; he has no choice.

'It's open, Dad. Really it is.'

'Is it?' He holds her wrist in his hand, wanting to believe. But they all lie to him now, and he has lost sight of the question of degree.

'The almond is about to flower.'

He reaches a hand up to the shelf by the bed: 'What about the wall? Where is the wall? I don't think it's safe.' His strength is all in his arms, built up almost unnoticed over half a century. The memory of it remains; he pushes against the wall.

Ruth moves the bed away from the wall, 'That's better, isn't it.' He feels the gap with his hand, 'Yes.'

They sit in silence; he goes on looking round the room.

'Where's your mother?'

'Sitting downstairs.'

'Resting, d'you think?'

'I expect so.'

They pause, looking at this other convenient fiction. There is no way to speak directly in the language that they share, to acknowledge that there is no rest for the woman downstairs while he dies so exhaustively. Ruth hopes that this does not matter; they know what they know.

Sometimes the need to communicate comes to him with unusual strength. He tries another avenue. 'She'd better be, hadn't she!' He smiles, an emaciated, wide smile.

✳

What're you going to do today?' Sam leans on an elbow, bringing the covers closer to her chin.

'Nothing,' Ruth says, turning over so that her face is buried in the pillow.

Sam gulps her coffee, eyeing the dirty, spiky hair next to her, 'Well, that's thrilling. I'll think about you doing nothing while I work.'

'You get paid for it, don't you?'

'I like working. You don't even like not working. You could be enjoying all this free time, and half the time you can't even be bothered to get up. That's what I can't stand to think about.'

Ruth rolls over, making an effort to stretch her face into the social semblance of a grin: 'But I like staying in bed.'

Sam sorts irritably through the hangers in the wardrobe, snapping them back and forth, 'I wish you'd drink your coffee. It's congealing.'

Ruth reaches her hand to the bedside table, wondering at the impulse that had brought her to this pass. It would have been less trouble to stay at home and sleep badly there.

'You were a nicer person when I first knew you.' Sam turns her back to pull on her underclothes. 'Less of a parasite.'

'Why're you wearing a bra?'

Sam pulls the buttons of her shirt together quickly, 'I'm not interested in symbolic gestures.'

Ruth drinks her coffee in silence. When Sam has finished dressing and is in the kitchen, making vague domestic sounds, Ruth lies back again and stares at the light fixture above her head. She calculates that in half-an-hour she will be able to get up and go home quietly.

Sam stands in the doorway: 'Come through and have breakfast with me.'

She thinks of Ruth as someone half-drowned to whom she can still throw a lifebuoy, if only for old times' sake.

'All right.' Ruth puts on the layers of her clothing, not quite daring to fight against another's hope.

The toast is neatly in the rack, the butter under a glass dome. 'I just bought a whole dinner service, decided I really liked matching plates. What d'you think?'

'Smart.' Ruth weighs the plate obediently in her hands, 'Better than that red plastic stuff we used to have.'

Sam laughs, 'And those huge army mugs, d'you remember?'

'What did you mean, a nicer person?' Ruth spreads marmalade thickly across her toast.

Sam lifts her arm in a vague, inclusive gesture: 'You're only half here, aren't you. If I want to speak to you, I have to make all the effort.'

'I came to see you last night.'

'For physical comfort with minimal effort.'

'To see an old friend.' Ruth is rather enjoying, rather hoping that such uncomplicated selfishness could be true, could be her true self.

'You don't have friends anymore, Ruth, just people who are used to you.' Sam's hands shake with a cleansing anger as she reaches into her handbag for a cigarette.

Ruth shrugs and bites into her toast. She seems to shrink slightly, as if something has deflated.

Sam watches her, eyes narrowed against the smoke. "I'd like to be friends with you, after all. I let you in, didn't I?'

'Not worth the effort, by the sound of it.' Ruth licks her finger and picks crumbs off her plate.

'I'm making one –'

'Maybe I'd rather you didn't.'

Ruth pushes her chair back gently. When she walks out, it is very quietly, as if she hopes that her departure might therefore go unnoticed.

✳

'You won't stay to supper?' It is irritating, that she must ask more than once.

'I ought to be back tonight, really.' Ruth leans in the kitchen window, staring out.

'Well, then.' Sadie is accustomed to not pressing herself upon others. Not one to waste energy in pursuit of a lost cause. Ruth lingers, eyes on the garden, as if there could be something out there that she might find hard to leave.

Sadie turns the dry crinkled leaves of her scrapbook, slowly, looking for small blue flowers. The chalk uplands, where the air is thin and the grass dry and sparse. Hard-won little flowers, insignificant in the great rolling landscape. That they are dried, pressed between the pages, hardly matters, already almost dessicated by the sharp chalk wind when she first takes them in her hand.

'Sorry.'

Sadie lifts her head from the book. Ruth is shifting from foot to foot, a parody of unease. It seems curious to Sadie that she should feel the need to apologise for her absence where it is not regarded. To David, indeed, she should be apologising, how does she justify the desertion to him? So few links remaining with the world, and she leaves him with a smile and a wave and the promise of return.

'Your father misses you.' You could leave me with a smile and a wave, any time, had you the grace to do it.

'I'll ring, in a few days.'

'He might be dead, in a few days.'

Ruth looks surprised, and sits down. The leaves of the scrapbook fall together.

'How do you know?'

'I don't, one way or the other.'

Sadie opens the book again, lowers her head to read the neatly printed details. *june fourteenth, clear weather, light SW wind. picked early morning, centre of large patch in west-facing hollow. ?dwarf form, or miniaturised by wind.*

Ruth scrapes dirt from under her fingernails.

'This has been going on so long.' Ruth has been waiting, for months. To know how she will feel when it happens.

Sadie looks at her sketch of tuberous roots. So long, they spread across the page. So much underpinning: she had sat in the sun and been set back, all over again, by the complexity of what lay underground, away from her sight. Long white roots spreading out, mocking her attempt at understanding.

'I can't stay, now.' Now it is much too late. He might already have died too many times.

The pages fall heavily, with a flat sound. Sadie leaves through toward late summer.

'It's up to you,' she says. Not wanting that Ruth should reveal her inner processes across the kitchen table. She would so much rather not learn of Ruth's struggles with her conscience. She lets another page turn: 'It's almost time for the four o'clock train.'

'Do you think he might really, in the next few days?'

Sadie shrugs: 'Who can say?' Her hands keep a place,

the time she is looking for. More plants here, inhabitants of windblown places. These the cliff-hangers, insecure. Thin little roots clinging to shifting rock. A scrabbling claw dislodges them, a landslip sends them tumbling down into the sea. Slowly, inexorably, as the coast crumbles they are flung aside.

'I don't know what to do –' Ruth's voice is only a murmur.

'Stay. Or go. Whichever you want.'

'I don't know.' Her head turns to a sound, 'Was that him calling?'

'Sounded like next-doors baby.'

'I think I'll go and check.'

Knowing him asleep, incapable of resisting the drugs so long, Sadie waits in silence, stooped at the kitchen table. Her eyes return to the neatly-pressed campion, thrift, wild pea. Falling gratefully from the cliff-face into her bag. Almost as if glad of the permanence she offered. How the wind howled, at the top there, as she clung to jutting rocks, knowing herself to be taking unnecessary risks. The same plants grew down below, could be reached from the path; but they had not the same savour. Crushed into her book they would not give off the same perfume as these, the hardiest of survivors.

Ruth looms into the kitchen: 'He's asleep.'

'Yes.'

Ruth stands inert, resting her hands on the table. It is as if they are all suspended somewhere between wakefulness and sleep, unable to fight clear of the cloying fog that is settling on the brain.

Ruth shakes her head, 'Have to go, I think.'

'I'll give you the fare.'

'It's all right.'

'I know you can't afford it.'

Ruth would like to cast the money away, to be made to pay for her departure. Financial suffering will serve: it is real and tangible, something she will surely feel, running short later in the week.

Sadie opens her bag. It seems filled with money these days, she is always taking more of the joint account in case there is something that he wants. She has taken to fulfilling needs at a moment's notice.

'I don't need as much as that.'

'Well, take a taxi at the other end. Or buy yourself something for supper.'

'Thanks,' Ruth stuffs the note into her pocket.

'Have a safe journey.' Sadie's hand strays back to the scrapbook. She smiles mildly.

'You'll let me know then?'

'I'll let you know, if there's a change.'

✳

'You're no good, you don't take it seriously.'

Toni looking her in the eye, dismissive.

'Too dangerous, going out with you.'

I can beat people up, Ruth wants to say, I'm quite dedicated there. But that, too, would be dangerous.

Toni standing in the road, half-laughing, her voice bitter-edged. Pulling the spoils out of Ruth's pockets.

'Smoked salmon, I suppose that's what you eat? You picked up a packet of crisps, wanted something good and crunchy to make a noise with, that it? Oh, you paid for the crisps. Christ, doesn't that make all the difference.'

A little heap spilt out onto the pavement at Ruth's feet.

'You don't know from nothing, do you? What did you want with the pastry cases, exactly?'

'Should we –' Ruth begins.

Toni sees the meaning in her eye: 'And there we are again, you're embarrassed, aren't you, standing in the road. You mustn't make an exhibition of yourself, what would the neighbours say?'

Toni stands back, weary.

'You are so fucking predictable. Do you know how tired it makes me sometimes, what it feels like?'

Ruth shakes her head, 'No.'

'Good,' Toni turns on her heel, 'you better not presume to understand.'

Halted by the roadside, Ruth eats the smoked salmon undiluted, straight from the wrapping. Toni bounces down the street, away from her.

'I'd like to see you lift a washing machine,' Toni says, taking it up again.

'Are they heavy?' Ruth asks, staring into her beer.

'Pinch one, stupid, I wonder where you are some of the time.'

'In a plastic bag,' Ruth mutters, 'against sensation.'

'You can afford to be.'

'What kind of dare is that, anyway?'

Toni looks at her, withering: 'You would take it as a dare, of course. It's just a little game to you, after all.'

'You've stolen a washing machine?'

'No, but I could if I had to.' Toni sighs, tilting her glass.

'And for christ sake don't go out and get me a washing machine just to prove how clever you are.'

'You wouldn't be touched?' Ruth asks.

'I'd be done for receiving stolen goods, idiot.'

✳

Ruth goes to the door in the shirt that passes for her nightdress. The milkman has broadened himself in the entrance. 'You owe me thirteen weeks.'

Ruth clasps her arms across her breast, 'I don't drink milk anymore. Not for a long time.'

He grins: 'It's too late. You already have.'

'Will part of it do?'

'Until next week.'

Ruth watches the float slide away from the curb. She tries to remember when she has ordered milk.

Carol is carrying groceries.

'I wouldn't open the door half-dressed,' she says, looking at the bare knees beneath the coat.

'I didn't know you were coming.'

Carol lifts her eyebrows, setting her parcels down beside the stove. She takes a small package off the top of her basket with both hands, 'I brought these for a treat.'

Ruth watches her, opening cupboards for a bowl, shaking out the fruit gently. The indecency of strawberries before spring. 'They must come from somewhere strange.'

Carol nods, sprinkling sugar with a flick of the wrist.

'I haven't seen you in a long time,' she says.

Ruth picks up a strawberry, 'The milkman said the same.'

'Shall I cook some vegetables for lunch?' Carol brings a heavy flowering of cauliflower out of her bag.

Ruth eyes it; such an object, so extensive. 'I've been all right.' She sits against the kitchen wall turning up the sleeves of her overcoat, watching Carol bent over the stove, chopping and stirring in the small space. A scene of rescue, of the deranged brought back from the brink by supportive hands.

'How's your father?'

'Oh, you know. Dying.' She helps herself from the bowl of strawberries, 'With dignity, etcetera.'

Carol pokes the cauliflower with a fork, 'I do feel for you.' Ruth laughs.

*

She has lain in bed all day, sleeping, waiting, drinking tea and pressing buttons on the radio. The news bulletins repeat themselves; she mouthes the familiar words. Each time signal brings the evening closer. Ruth has forgotten that there might be any other purpose to the day, wanting only the streets, the dark, the flat sound of her soft shoes on pavement.

Finally she gets up, moving backwards and forwards across the room, her nightdress dim in the half-light. The clothes are laid out on the bed. Ruth pulls the nightdress over her head, a sudden, ritual motion. Two layers of cotton, familiar, fraying at the edges: against the cold, against the cold sweat that will prick at her, standing in shadows, or hearing a noise at her back. So then the tracksuit, dark and loose. A thousand of them out there now, running aimlessly in suits like these. Running to nowhere. On Ruth an instrument, loose enough for more than mere running. The leather jacket, its lining cool and slippery, guiding her hands. The leather smooth, smelling of saddle soap worked into every crevice. So that it shall not tear, shall shrug off hands, blows, protect her from the biting asphalt. Ruth snaps the fasteners, moves to look at herself in the mirror. They cannot see what she wears, those out there, the purpose of it staring out at them. Her protection a population that cannot read the signs she carries.

The thin gloves hang limp and malleable in her hand; she smoothes them on. The last disguise settles over her. As she pulls on the black shoes Ruth's movements seem to change, to become smoother, slightly distanced from the norm. As if she follows the steps of a dance.

She walks, always, because it is unbearable to be separated from the immediacy of the ground, the pavement. She needs to see everything, cannot risk the bus's speed that might carry her past the crucial scene. She walks, trying to see how the night is, the feel of it. She might be trying to smell it, savour it, try it on her tongue for violent or peaceful, sniff the quality of danger. At the corner of the street, Elsie's house in sight, she relaxes a little, stopping under a street light to breathe. Half-aware that she must not be seen there, so lit-up and so wide awake.

✷

She rarely speaks to people behind counters, in the city. An attempt at politeness seems to surprise them, coming from her, and she will have to stand, suspended, while they look her up and down and consider how to respond. And so Ruth averts her eyes, passing the ticket across the counter, mutters her shoe size and follows the pointing arm.

The changing room is cavernous and oddly silent. Outside, all round the rink, there are screeching clusters of children, boys with violent hands, the shrill hysteria of people who have lost control of their bodies. In here there is quiet, men lacing up their boots with intense fingers.

Ruth's breath fogs the air, as cold here as on the ice. She sits on the end of a bench, brown boots dangling from her hand. Time was when her boots were white, her own and only secondhand. The stuff of legend, your first pair of skates. Carefully whitened, feet of snow. Long gone and not replaced when the feet grew larger than size three. She has had her chance, it seems, and not taken it. She runs her finger along the edge of the blades: it is not with these that she will jump the highest barrier, or skate the frozen river from end to end.

Ruth focuses on the man across the room who stands on a bench, looking out over the floor. As Ruth watches he unzips his clinging nylon suit and rolls it down past his knees. Unhurried, he takes a towel from his bag and begins to rub the sweat from his body, a rasping sound in the quiet. Ruth considers him, naked and steaming in the cold air. Her gaze flicks about the room. Other men, professionals in states of undress, small boys combing their hair, a few lads unsteady on their feet, ankles bending, and herself: the men's changing room. Ruth puts her boots gently down on the bench and bends to unlace her shoes.

The shoes give nothing away. Ruth concentrates on her feet, on the business of fitting her skates, tightening laces. They are not noticing the trembling in her hands. She stands up, measuring the distance to where she must hand over her shoes. A long stride, loose, down on the waterfront. Running her hand through her hair. Waiting for the ticket, an atonal grunt as he passes it over.

In the corridor Ruth leans against the wall, letting her heart slow. Ahead of her, on the ice, a waltz is overlaid with the screams of girls clinging to the barrier. She walks toward them, past the women's changing room that she cannot enter. It might be warmer in there, and full of girls in their leotards eating crisps, but she has been debarred. They would look her up and down and notice the colour of her boots. They would point her back down the corridor, giggling as the door closed.

The young women are absorbed, grasping at one another and watching their feet slide away from under them with shrieks of surprise. Ruth glides past them, skates acknowledging the ice with relief. This is simple, an old trick of balance and grace that her body remembers without complications. She sways lightly to and fro, pushing forward, taking speed. She finds the inside and begins to circle, leaning inward, the cries of the stranded coming to her in straggling bursts as she sweeps past them, wind in her ears.

Gradually, more people come onto the ice and Ruth finds she cannot ignore them, must weave in and out, brushing between groups, swerving round a body cascaded onto the ice in front of her. Yet she is at a great distance, circling them alone. Almost touching as she passes, she is effortlessly cut off from them all. Ruth skates through the press of the crowd with bitterness and precision.

STREET SCENE: THREE

They have gathered earlier tonight, the four of them, such as they are. As if to prove that they still may have effect, that no diminution can deny them. Tam, circled upon herself in her chair, emanated indifference to inessential changes. It is enough that she will be out there, wielding herself against the world.

'We waiting for something?'

Sheila dangles her hands between her knees: 'You can't wait to get out there, can you.'

'I'm supposed to be reluctant?'

Elsie puts the tray of coffee squarely down on the table, 'We don't want eagerness.'

Lying on the settee Gloria lifts her head, wary.

The grate of another key in the lock, and they all turn to the door. Knowing that it will be Ruth, unable to stay away.

'Why are you here? There isn't a partner for you.' Elsie stands across her path.

Ruth leans in the doorway, her leather arms folded. 'Thought I might replace someone. Might be ill, or something.' She studies the floor, the edges of the room, the fringes of the rug.

'We would've let you know, you know that.' Elsie does not move, as if to do so will be to let her in, unattached and dangerous, too ready for the streets.

'She can come with us.'

Sheila glances round at Sue, sitting beside her: 'No, she can't.'

'Too conspicuous, even for you nice white girls.' Tam stands up suddenly.

'Why don't you go on, all of you.' Elsie gestures them through the door. They pass carefully, not allowing clothes to touch.

'Why did you come?' Elsie steps back, letting her into the empty room.

'I wanted to.'

'You have to get used to staying at home. Until we find someone to go out with you.'

Ruth shrugs. 'I don't do any harm, being here.'

Elsie sighs, sitting down. 'I've got some cuttings. D'you want to look at them?'

Sue kicks a tin can away from her, shattering long silence. It careens off the sides of the tunnel, a high-pitched, rattling echo.

'You make too much noise.' Sheila shivers at the cold of the concrete reaching her back.

'Nothing happens down here anymore.' She looks down to flick lint from the sleeve of her jacket.

The sodium glare of the lights outlines their breath. Sheila stares into the orange glow.

'What d'you mean?'

Sue leans back against the wall, closing her eyes: 'Nobody gets jumped down here, haven't you noticed?'

'It's too cold.'

'It's always cold down here.'

Sheila looks up and down, a quick flick of the head, 'I never liked this fucking underpass.'

'What d'you think this does to the nerves?' Tam is bouncing, her feet leaving the ground at every stride.

Gloria grins: 'Life is bad for the nerves.'

'I could be enjoying myself.'

'Instead of prowling the streets with Mama Gloria the avenging angel.'

'Maybe I want to choose who I protect.'

They turn the corner into the arcade, a spread of wide empty paving. As they walk they are watching the shadows, the pillars, the doorways.

'Well, that's different.'

Gloria pauses, her hand out to Tam's sleeve; she nods into the distance, at a faint trace of movement.

'You don't have to look after the world, just because I do.'

There is a sudden sound of breaking glass, a shape leaping in front of them and sprinting away.

'We could go finish his thieving?'

Gloria keeps hold of her arm: ‘And who’s going to get picked up for it?’

‘I know. And who am I putting my life on the line for?’ Gloria turns her round, the way they have come.

‘I was brought up a baptist. We would say we were instruments of the Lord.’

Tam laughs as they run back down the street, the burglar alarm screaming behind them.

SOURCE MATERIAL: SUE

There can be so little harm in a banana. Surely, very little harm. But she cannot remember the constituent properties. The book is in the kitchen, with the banana. This could be the mania of earliest morning, twisting her mind: bananas as vicious as peanuts, innocent handfuls that spread and grow in the body, lining their fatty selves along the arteries, layering themselves into immobile fatty tissue. Thighs swell, ballooning at the thought. The banana is a mascarade, a stalking horse: no sooner in the kitchen than her hands would grow to sucking tentacles, reaching out concentrated as an octopus to cram and thrust into her mouth. Mouth, she is all mouth, lying in the bed opening and closing slow lips. In the kitchen the tentacles are past discrimination, grasp earthy potatoes, take glass jars and crumple them for the juices inside. The shelves will be bare in a moment, the floor a litter of glass shards and tumbled plants. The vandal mouth roves and searches, its strength relentless. It heaves aside the cooker, the refrigerator, groping in the dust behind for grease and crumbs, the neglected debris. Unsated, surrounded by destruction, it turns and turns, its grunt rising slowly to a scream.

Sue sleeps, the exhausted sleep of starvation. Chilled, her body hunkers desperately into the blankets.

Sunlight reaching into the room brings her awake. At once, under the blankets, she is aware of lightness. She feels with her hand the concave pit of her stomach, the jut of her hip bones. It is falling away. She lies still, pushing away the ice at her feet, the shivering in her legs. The body exists without needs now, clear and light as the early morning. It lies beneath her hand without demands. Sue stares into the low, white sun.

But the body cries to be warm, just that, to be clothed and heated. Sue bends herself to listen, considering the supplicant prone on the marble before her. It is humble and asks for little. She decides that it pleases her to comply. She reaches a consoling hand to the tousled hair: arise, my child, I shall grant your request. You are so pale and fragile, pitiable.

The happy skeleton swings its legs to the edge of the

bed, gingerly and not all at once against the danger of faintness at a too-sudden movement. It prances with just a little discretion across the room on numb feet, eager to reach the wardrobe. Rows of white sliding doors, enigmatic. The appearance of an empty room: behind the thin white shell lies another layer of space, shelves and hanging cupboards. Open any door and enter the hidden region. The skeleton pushes back one of the doors with its large hands, steps inside. The dresses hang here in racks; they sway and click to its touch. The thin fingers stroke material, rub against velvet, sensation transmitted with new intensity. But cold, too cold. Step backwards from the cupboard and pass on. Open other doors, pick over the stacked shelves. The skeleton's hands peer and pry, searching. Finally clasp to its bony chest the padded trousers, warm with layers of cotton quilting. Against the breast bone the heat radiates. Limbs quiver, fitting themselves into layers of silk underwear, all that the sensitive bones can bear. The skeleton wreathes its adam's apple in scarves, pulls ties at the trouser ends. Stands at last padded against the world.

Sue looks at herself in the bathroom mirror. The whites of her eyes leap back at her, almost blue with purity. She applies colour to her cheekbones. She pushes the heavy silver circlet up her left arm.

The refrigerator is green and lustrous with bottles of mineral water. They quiver, a sylvan glade reflecting muted light. Sue places green bottle and stemmed glass on the table. Their shadows lean across the surface, a still life. Sue looks around the room, at a moment arrested: sunlight glints on the quiet rows of glass, on the gloss of cupboard doors. Sue lifts her hand to the bottle, tilts sparkling water into the glass. She becomes part of the picture: a young woman seated sideways on a chair, her clothes carefully layered, her face side-lit, emphasising the fine bones.

The window glisters. Sue toys with resistance, considers moving on without a backward glance. The window reaches out: so many possibilities.

The carpet curls up to meet her ankles, heat floats from the draped corners of the room. The arum lilies in the black vase nod slightly as the door closes. The woman behind the desk flicks back her waxy hair and smiles. Sue drops her bag on the floor, acknowledging herself welcomed. The rich, blonde hair is expansive: there is all the time you require.

Sue is mesmerised by softness, by soft lightness. The idea that fabric will hang close to her, cling or shift, layers of gentle sensation. She lays hands upon the samples and they back gently away from her along the rails as if escaping coyly from her embrace.

The woman stands at the door of the changing room, the captured clothes lying passive across her arm. She watches, distant, as Sue unwraps herself of layers. Sue turns slowly before the mirrors. She bends to unlace the ties of her trousers. The woman at the door shifts, passing her hand through her hair.

Almost unclothed, now, in the centre of the small room. At the door a slight movement, of the arm or hand. Sue takes the first item from the pile. Her attention on the glowing thing in her hand, she does not feel the strangeness, standing quite revealed before the onlooker. Whose eyes consider her.

Experienced, she at the door admires the denial that has culminated in attenuated flesh, the clear pattern of ribs as she stands waiting. If she were to raise her arms they would be yet more defined, the detail tangible beneath a thin skin. There are dark hollows at the throat, at the meeting of the collar bones. Pools of darkness.

Sue flings the dress over her head, casts it across the room. The woman at the door holds out the next, forbearing. Sue slides into it, tossing tousled hair out of her eyes. Stands, hand on hip. It fails to please, hanging limp from her bones. The dresser shifts the stack on her arm, draws out another. Sue steps over the crumpled heaps, taking the dress warily; it too might turn its fragile self against her. But the woman smiles, as if all this is only to be expected, a necessary preliminary rite.

Sue stares into the mirror as the dark material settles onto her. She looks over, surrendering herself.

The woman gestures: 'Turn around.'

Sue turns herself in a circle, slowly.

'Faster, turn faster.'

The dress begins to lift and sway. Sue smiles, watching the animated thing in the mirror that twirls itself into life. At the door she nods: it is suitable. Flaring material, shadowed hollows of the body. She turns away abruptly, letting the curtain fall across the entrance. Alone, Sue eddies to a stop.

Sue sits on the edge of the desk, swinging her stockinged feet. She is still wearing the dress, unwilling to abandon the game at which she has succeeded. The other leans back in her chair, allowing herself admiration. Knowing how animation is sustained, she pours cups of black coffee. At last, at the directness of her stare, Sue slips back behind the curtain, folding the dress to her.

The dress lies ready, woven into tissue paper in its bag. They look at one another fleetingly, sidelong, through filtered eyes.

*

It is the usual thing. They are wearing fancy dress and everyone is carrying a glass of champagne in each hand. Parties have always been like this, there is really no help for it. Custom demands becoming as drunk as possible and speaking loudly. Upstairs in the master bedroom the financiers and their mistresses will be taking expensive drugs. Men dressed as harleguins swarm the room, searching for release.

A man in women's clothing stands at the buffet table, sucking up oysters. The heels to his shoes are very high; his skirt is tightly moulded to his buttocks and thighs.

He has the air of someone who does this often. A shepherdess, her breasts uplifted and revealed, picks almonds from the top of the dishes of paté. Sue stands by the ice buckets, methodically filling and draining her glass. She is wearing black leather and carrying a regimental sword at her belt.

'Very cordon blurr, this, isn't it.' A harlequin offers the shepherdess fondue on a stick of celery.

'Was I at school with you?'

A guardsman elbows his way towards the oysters, treading on the toes of the man in high heels.

'What are you?' he asks, noticing the sword.

The shepherdess smiles and bends her swan neck to crunch celery between white teeth.

'There's something so immoderate about oysters.'

'A highwaywoman,' Sue says, gulping back the champagne in her right hand.

A woman wearing white tie and tails sorts critically through the ice buckets with small slender hands. She puts the full bottle that she finds under her coat. Sue watches her thread her way through the crowd towards the front door.

'Did you see Deirdre's got herself up as a hedgehog? All too true –'

'I don't suppose you could hold this for me?' Swathed all over in bandages, he needs both hands to manipulate the bottle of champagne over his glass.

'I take it you're a leper?' Sue takes the proffered glass.

'Hadn't thought about that.'

Two boys dressed as ice maidens float across the floor, arms linked. Cleopatra, her skin colour beading at her temples, dances by herself, braceleted arms crossed over her chest.

'And you?'

'This is my third this week, did you know?'

'Very influential, those places they send you as a child.'

'The black sheep, of course.' Sue leans toward him, 'Wouldn't it be easier just to put the bottle in your mouth?'

He giggles into the bandages.

A gloved hand insinuates itself smoothly between them. The black silk mask considers her: 'Quite similar, don't you think.'

His leather has the patina of use.

'I'm here as a rapist.' He smiles.

'I'm the castrating woman,' Sue says, stepping round him.

'I hope you're not going to make me stop eating oysters.' The man in heels looks appealingly into the rapist's mask. Sue administers a second bottle to the man in bandages. On the cushions in the corner of the room two harlequins have the shepherdess between them.

A wrapped sweet, frills of starchy paper at neck and knees, is shuffling about the room looking for the matador with whom she arrived. A sailor, following her, offers to untie the tight bonds clamping her calves.

Sue and the bandaged man walk up the stairs, hand in hand. At the turn of the stairs a cossack is leafing through a stack of magazines, outdoor and pornographic. They walk along the corridor, opening and shutting doors. On the second floor they find a child's room, stuffed pink rabbit laid out on the bedspread.

The wrapped sweet leans into the arms of the sailor.

'You just lie down and I'll unwind you.' Her voice is honey. He sighs as Sue unpins the first bandage.

The ice maidens sit disconsolate on the terrace, shivering. No one has asked them to dance.

His skin is mottled pink and white from the pressure. Cascades of bandage curl to the floor beside the narrow bed.

'I hope you're enjoying this.' She bends to unfasten the pin at his ankles.

The rapist finds himself catching the man in high heels as he lurches, scattering oyster shells across the floor. The body is surprisingly light against him; he wonders whether it is a man after all.

The guardsman is in the kitchen discussing the psychological effects of basic training with the host, who is as usual dressed as the sun king. They agree that it does more harm than good.

He is satisfyingly naked under the bandages. She unwinds slowly and he smiles, watching her. At last he springs erect from the last bandage. Sue unbuttons her trousers.

'Aren't you going to take off your sword?' She settles herself on top of him.

The sailor takes the wrapped sweet outside to look for a taxi. Her tears are staining his hired costume.

The ice maidens waltz on the terrace, ignoring the muttered insults of the cossack.

'What did you say you were?' He snuggles his bare feet into the candlewick, sleepily.

'An avenging angel.' Sue slides off the bed, gathering bandages into her arms.

The shepherdess, sobbing in the kitchen, is given cups of strong tea by the hostess, who wears an apron over her glittering silver lame.

The wrapped sweet drives away in her taxi, waving.

Sue thrusts the heap of bandages into the hands of the ice maidens. Their mouths open soundlessly.

The cossack drives his car into a lamp post on the outskirts of the city.

The guardsman walks, alone and unaccountably sober.

The boy ice maidens wrap bandages gently about one another and smile.

The moon, still wearing her apron, looks down coldly at the flushed naked man in the pink room.

*

The waiter coils himself around the table. Margery smiles warmly into his eyes, 'My friend can order for me.' She is unconcerned to expose her limitations, trusting that she will be forgiven and understood. The waiter's eyelids flicker. He turns his face to her companion, raising his notepad.

Sue orders without inflexion.

Margery fiddles with the glassware, watching rainbow refractions splinter across the tablecloth. She absorbs every detail of her surroundings, a rich cake of layered impressions to be stored away. She notices the density of the linen on her plate, the calling song of the diners at other tables, the flick of black and white as the waiters pass between them.

She admires, as one might a photograph, the woman sitting across from her; the lines are sculpted, the fingers wrapped casually about a glass, the head elegantly tilted, the eyes distant. In her mind she is already at home, bringing back the tapestry, pointing out highlights: you wouldn't've known her, so city and so mysterious.

'Tell me about yourself, Sue.'

'Upper-class girl gone bad, Margery.' Sue's lips lift into the essay of a smile.

Margery twitches her nostrils for the scent of dissipation. Her eager eyes run over the stretched skin and bone of Sue's face. The facade stares back out at her, uncommunicative. She searches her memory for the seeds of destruction. It is true that she remembers Sue walking along the sea wall when an east wind was throwing the waves against the buttresses, sending spray thirty feet into the air. She remembers Sue standing in the midst of the spray, drenched and shouting. She remembers Sue at the cliff top, balancing on the updraft, her hair streaming out behind her.

'You always liked danger,' she says.

Sue's hand clenches on the stem of her glass, her shoulders stiffen. She wonders at Margery's powers of observation.

'At school,' Margery adds.

'Oh, at school –' Sue shrugs, casting away the excesses of adolescence, 'other forms of indulgence these days.'

Margery takes in further the evidences offered to her, of wealth freely consumed in the purchase of things transitory. It seems insufficient to describe a life. She has remembered how difficult Sue was inclined to be, how hard to satisfy about anything. How much she disliked almost everyone. How she liked to tease people about the absurdity of their cherished beliefs, relentless until she had reduced them to tears or screaming rages.

'Not married, then?'

Sue smiles: 'Not ready to settle down quite yet.'

'You used to be rather tempestuous.'

'Did I?'

'You can't have forgotten.'

Sue allows herself to blink once, as a lizard turns aside a stare, 'Must have. I remember this huge draughty building filled with large girls of extraordinary innocence. And having to change one's clothes a great many times a day.'

'That was just the place.'

'It's what I remember.'

Margery looks into the smooth face. By comparison she is seamed and craggy, lines at the corner of her mouth that imitate crevasses. So many places to take hold.

'I remember you playing that prince, or whatever he was.'

'A knight. And you were my lady.'

'That sword –' A pallid young knight in cream-coloured tights, but with that sword and the matching yellow hair, and the way she drew herself up and looked down upon you with undisguised contempt, almost too real. Margery recalled how exposed she had felt, held on stage in those thin, unforgiving arms.

'I didn't have a sword.'

'Yes, you did. And you wore it round school all the next day, as well.'

The waiter lays plates down in front of them, splashes of colour isolated on the brilliant white expanse, the sparsest of abstracts. Margery lifts her hands to her face, a small, joyful gesture. She barely restrains a cry of rapture. With fearful delicacy her fork descends upon the feast of colour.

Sue watches with relief as Margery wings away on a sensory exploration, eyes widening, mouth opening and closing, every fibre concentrated upon layer after layer of taste sensation. She has no wish to open to Margery's probing, to be called to the task of explaining herself to this alien person. If she has arrived at some odd accommodation with the world, its oddity does not become less because Margery tries to understand it.

Gradually, her plate empty, Margery drifts to a halt. The food she has just eaten is so entirely different from that to which she is accustomed that she is conscious almost of pain, that she should have been introduced to something which the daily reality of her life will not allow her to encounter ever again. She comprehends with a new intensity the existence of other worlds than her own. Margery rests her hands at the side of her plate, shocked at the perfection of what she has just consumed.

The gauze drawn briefly back from her eyes, she observes Sue's casual, cold picking at her plate with anger. The affectation of indifference can only be yet another refinement, the search for still greater decadence. Sue has again managed to invalidate her experience, turn Margery's joy to ashes in her mouth in her swift espousal of more ethereal things. As hatred wells up, locked regions of memory reveal themselves to her.

'You used to like Jack the Ripper, didn't you.'

'Did I?'

'You used to say you were a reincarnation of Jack the Ripper.'

'All children go through phases.'

'Of identifying with murderers?'

Smoothly the table is emptied and again filled with plates, more sculptured artifacts laid out on dazzling white grounds. Margery opens her mouth and finds that her savour for the food has returned. She looks with brief pity on Sue whose eyes are averted, not welling with the mind's feast spread before her. As she passes each morsel across the harp of her taste buds, Margery preserves with careful attention a sense of where the conversation has been interrupted. Only when nothing remains to provide sublime distraction does she resume.

'Do you remember, liking Jack the Ripper?'

'You were always easy to shock.'

'You used to go on, about drawing the knife down the abdomen and dragging out the guts.'

'Did I?'

'You used to say, shall I show you what he did.'

'Children like horror, I remember you rather enjoying it.'

'You used to admire him.'

Sue looks at Margery's well-padded body, hunched at the other side of the table. It is surprising, given that physical appearance, to see her revealed as a vulture circling to pick at bones.

'You wanted to be like him, you said.'

Sue waves a hand irritably: 'Because he was successful, I suppose.'

'Successful?'

'I mean, of course, that he was never found out. Only a schoolgirl fantasy.'

The waiter stands at her side. 'We will have the pear sorbet.' Sue says, turning again to Margery. 'It is exquisite, the eternal essence of pear.'

Margery blinks, seeing her quarry start up suddenly and twist away, weaving and turning.

'So what do you do, that I mustn't find out?' And she smiles, a warm country smile.

Sue's strength is that she can remain motionless for hours, a basilisk against a concealing background. She waits, now, for the coming of the dessert as if she had not heard.

STREET SCENE: FOUR

They are there, waiting. As it happens Sheila realises that she is not surprised, has known it coming to her. She has only chosen to turn away her head, allowing herself a little recklessness.

Sue is sauntering, bored, her eyes focused on the rough niche they always occupy, her shoulders anticipating the discomfort of the wall.

'Doesn't the night seem long,' she says.

Sheila grunts. As they draw abreast of the dark corner there is a sudden leap of colour, thrown towards them. Sheila's breath hisses out: they become three men, their mouths open in cries that echo down the underpass, their faces white and too close.

Sheila finds herself with her back to the wall, two of them about her. At the corner of her eye she catches Sue and the other one, circling. In the slowed moment it seems to her that she can probably hold them off for quite a while, that there is always the possibility that they will lose interest. Sue circles, feeling a pure, simple excitement. Her limbs shiver and burn.

Sheila lashes out; they retreat perhaps half a step, grins spreading across their faces. She realises their dedication, that they have no intention of leaving.

He stretches long arms out toward her; Sue twitches, aside and aside. He reaches forward again, to grasp. Sue twists, cinematic, grabbing the arm. He stumbles and falls sharply onto his knees. Crunch of bone on concrete. Sue steps back, admiring.

'Run, then, what're you waiting for?' Sheila's voice sounds sudden and unfamiliar.

Sue turns without thought, running through the underpass, along the streets yellow with rain reflecting street lights, into the hedged by-ways where the trees drip. Pausing at last, gasping, against a wall, leaning there as her body begins to shake.

'Bastard,' says the man on his knees.

The others look at one another, shifting their feet across the cold floor.

'Get her then, you bastards.'

Sheila visualises a strategic strike, and then running, perhaps the need of the moment bearing her knee up, mind over tissue. She pushes herself from the wall.

Half-a-mile away Sue sits in the gutter, head between her knees. She has, finally, the taste of terror, welling behind clenched teeth. She rolls it across her palate like a new wine.

When Sheila tries to leave she is restrained, determined hands grip her arms. Her knee would not have held her anyway, she realises, staggering so that they have to hold her up. There is a detached quality to their actions as they press her against the wall; as if their concerns are scientific or otherwise impersonal.

The third man levers himself from the ground; his pain blossoms easily into anger. He begins to batter at the captured body, his head held to one side, listening for the crack of ribs. He stands so close to her, almost touching, a deliberate intimacy of violence.

Sue begins to run back the way she thinks to have come. Absurd, to be lost in these streets that she knows, her adoptive territory. She runs on, expecting the return of knowledge at each corner.

Tiring, he sucks blood away from his grazed knuckles. They let her fall to the ground, face against the cold ridged concrete. The man whose knees are painfully bruised is helped away along the underpass. Left alone Sheila breathes shallow, waiting without expectation for the sight of Sue's legs, thin and rapid on the ramp.

SOURCE MATERIAL: TAM

Tam tangles herself about the railings, irridescent green against iron. On the other side the noise continues, they hurl themselves upon each other, separate again, wheel across the asphalt. Tam's camera clicks and whirrs. A child twitches in its path, juddering to a halt. It stares at Tam, grasshopper sprawled and clicking.

They begin to gather, bunching together, keeping a certain distance. Tam takes pictures as they converge.

'Why you taking photos?'

They look her up and down. Some turn away, as if already afraid of the lens.

Tam lowers the camera: 'For a project, I have to take pictures of kids.'

They begin to recreate themselves for her, waving, gesticulating, distorting their faces. Tam raises the lens to her eye. The camera accepts indifferently the childrens' images of themselves, the refusals of those who turn their backs, the play of cold intermittent sunlight on the railings.

Tam breaks off suddenly, turning aside, unpicking her limbs and tacking off across the street. Behind her they gather at once where she has been, yelling and calling, their hands pushing through the bars.

Tam turns into the high street, pauses at the kerb. She waits to see whether the traffic detours round her. She lifts the camera to her eye and a cyclist swerves. When he looks back Tam is grinning, the camera weighed lightly in one hand.

In the darkroom Tam stands over the trays breathing fumes. She feels the numbness spreading outwards from the back of her head, like drinking too much, too quick, seizing the brain. She flicks the print backwards and forwards, watching the black leap across the paper. The children in the playground loom out towards her, a gargoyle mass of faces.

'I have this place booked from three, you know.'

Mary leans brightly against the wall, plastic folders clasped in her arms.

'Ten minutes.'

Tam begins to pile things into the dryer. Somehow she has let Mary back in with her, sitting with her skirt tucked up on the bench.

'I don't know why you don't do your photo-journalism assignments in colour.'

Mary squints at the prints going into the drier.

'I like to make things look nasty.'

'Blood looks nastier in colour.'

Tam would like so much to bring something hard down on her head, to see if blood looks different under the orange glow of the safelight. She stretches her arms above her head, a last gulp of developer into her lungs.

'How would you know?'

'I thought you were going.'

'It's you that's not going anywhere.' Tam walks out dancing, leaving the door wide, prancing down the stairs. She stalks along the street making the crowd part in front of her. She sees the bus coming, just too near so that she ought to run to catch it. She glares down the road. The bus traps itself behind a parked car so that Tam can reach the stop in safety, walking at her own pace.

*

'You going to go see her?' Eileen jams the fish slice under the potatoes in the pan, sending splinters flying.

'No.' Tam lifts her fork languidly to her face and peers through it.

'She's your grandmother.'

Tam turns the fork against the waxed plastic, digging, 'Not if she could help it.'

'Well she can't, can she. She's got to do with it.'

Eileen turns the potatoes again, not letting them rest.

'Like shit she has.'

'Leave the table alone, for chrissake.'

Tam lines her knife and fork up parallel, sits up in her chair, 'I'm not going.'

'She asks about you.'

Eileen tries the plates for warmth on the back of her

hand. She sorts the food into two. Spreading it out to fill the plate, an old habit.

'Lamb chop – you never used to give me lamb chop.'

'It's cheaper when I only see you once a month, isn't it. You never noticed what you ate anyway.'

Eileen pauses, head forward, looking under her eyebrows, to watch Tam eating. Each time she comes back she seems taller, thinner. Eileen wonders sometimes what she does with her body, to stretch it. Hangs from telegraph poles in the middle of the night, maybe.

'I hate that old woman and she hates me.'

'She's getting over it.'

'I'll send her a photo to put on her bedside table.'

Eileen waves her fork at the wall, 'Not one of these, she can't stand them.'

'I don't know how you can, it's abnormal. They're meant to make you jump in the river.'

Tam's photographs paper the walls They date back years, some of them, to when she first started at school, the camera an instrument of rape. Images of something she thought, then, had simply gone unnoticed: decaying buildings, the city degenerating. Crushed waitresses leaning on smeared tables, people walking the streets without purpose. If she is still taking the same pictures it is now to record a deliberately created world; every face has its own stain, the hatred marked. Eileen looks up at them briefly, 'That's how it is, isn't it. I like to know someone's seeing it.'

'Pity you couldn't tell your mother.'

And they sit in silence with this between them, the old woman who hates Tam more, who is insatiable and tireless.

*

Through the first door, and the smell changes. An odour of ether, rubber, piss. The second set of doors open into the entrance hall. There is no one there, but the place is full of sound echoing down from the corridors that splinter off in all directions. Screechings, and the blur of a television set on full volume, and the crashing of thin steel pans, and a high wailing, and voices raised in command.

Someone stalks down the corridor toward her carrying a bucket full of some pinkish liquid.

'You can't come now. It's lunch.' She turns, a precise three quarters turn, and disappears.

Tam waits, fingering the shiny chrome surface of her camera. A door slams, cutting off the wailing. The trolley bearing down on her rattles with pills and syringes.

'What do you want?' The trolley wheels slide to a halt, a foot away.

'To see my grandma.'

'Oh yes?' She raises her eyebrows, thick black ridges across the bleached white of her face.

'Ada Pearson.'

'You're hers, are you?' The white face cracks apart suddenly into an enormous yell of laughter. She jerks the trolley round and moves off down the corridor, the sound of her cackling receding slowly.

Tam sticks out her tongue, 'Piss off, why don't you.'

She goes over to the empty reception desk and kicks it. After a moment she walks round to the other side: all the drawers are locked shut, nothing is left exposed. Tam's fingers find a bell embedded in the underside of the desk top. She presses it. Somewhere in the far distance another noise begins, a discordant ringing. Tam sits down behind the desk and closes her eyes.

'I suppose you pressed the alarm?'

The woman standing in front of her is wearing a pink suit. Frills of pink blouse are thrust out at throat and wrist. Her thin arms lean across the desk.

'Yeh. There was no one here.'

'We are not open to visitors, except at certain hours of the afternoon.'

'I've come to see my grandma.'

Tam and the pink suit look at one another, measuring.

'Well, your grandma will be eating her lunch just now.'

'Doubt it. Expect she's complaining about it, or something.'

The pink suit folds her arms across her chest, 'We don't have many complaints about the food here.'

'Complains a lot, my grandma.'

'Are you making an official complaint?'

'What?'

'Have you received a complaint about our catering?'

'I haven't seen her yet, have I.'

The pink suit comes round behind the desk: 'You shouldn't be sitting in that chair.'

'I'm waiting to see my grandma.'

'Well, you can't wait here.'

'Why not?'

The pink suit places her hand on the chair. Tam notices the knuckles whitening. She bounces up, begins to circle the room at a lope, extending her long legs in wide strides.

'I'll just have to hang about then.'

'I haven't the time to spend making sure you don't get up to no good.' She stands unmoving, a hunter watching the movements of its prey.

Tam stops abruptly. She turns towards the pink suit and lifts the camera to her eye. Her face disappears behind the long black lens.

'You can't use that in here.' She lifts her finger and shakes it at Tam: 'Photographs are not allowed.'

A sudden crash reverberates towards them, overlaid by a highpitched keening. The pink suit's head snaps round, centres itself accurately on one of the corridors. She leaves without looking back.

Tam moves down one of the corridors, treading quietly in her soft-soled shoes. The doors are numbered in some pattern that she does not understand. She pushes one that is slightly ajar and finds herself looking at a row of open cubicles. Water drips from showerheads onto the slick tiled floor. She turns the handle of the next room with care. When she opens the door a fraction there is no sound. She steps inside and meets the stare of the old woman whose bed faces the door. She is propped up on pillows, her hands placed inert on the counterpane. They look at one another: the dark eyes in the yellow face require that Tam advance further into the room.

'You've been a long time coming,' the eyes study Tam as if they would pick her apart, 'whoever you are.'

'I've come to see my grandma.' Tam closes the door behind her and smiles, a polite smile.

'Not me.'

'No.'

'But here you are.' One hand moves very slightly, the sketch of a gesture, 'As I expected.'

'Someone's coming to visit you, then?'

'Don't talk to me in that tone, as if I were a child. You can leave if you're going to speak to me like that.'

'Sorry.'

Tam crosses to the window, two steps in the tiny space, a segment of what would once have been a single room.

'There's no view, I remember. You're not looking at anything.' Tam looks out on a patch of grass, muddy with winter, and a sheer brick wall, windowless and without feature.

'I'm right, aren't I. I used to look out too, when I could walk. Can't think why. Obviously someone's coming to visit, as you're here, or don't you count yourself as somebody? That won't get you anywhere, take it from me.'

Tam leans her head on the window pane, begins to bump her forehead rhythmically against the glass.

'Not very good value, are you. Must be losing my touch, to make up someone without a tongue in their head.'

'You didn't make me up,' Tam says, turning round to look at her accusingly.

'Didn't I?'

She looks at Tam consideringly, 'That colour is a bit inventive for me.' She glances down at her hands, curled and bloodless. 'What are you here for, then?'

'To see my grandmother, I told you.'

'Why?'

Tam stares at her, head moving from side to side on the pillow.

'It isn't done much here.'

Tam makes a sudden step to the bed: 'I want to have it out with her, sod the old bastard.'

'Well, think of that.' For the first time the old woman's eyes are vague, inward. 'I don't know how long it is since I heard anyone swear, you almost forget what the words are.'

'Shit, bugger, piss,' Tam adds helpfully, her anger diverted.

'Oh yes, those are good ones. They're too genteel to swear at me here, you know. Nasty, but genteel.' She grins widely at Tam, revealing the toothlessness of her mouth. 'So you don't get on with your grandmother.'

'She hates me.'

But the old woman is losing interest, wearying of her creation, 'Is she an ambulatory?'

'What?'

She waves her head, impatient, 'Can she walk? Not had a stroke, for instance?'

'I suppose so, how should I know?'

'Ambulatories are in the common room, third corridor on your right.'

'Goodbye then.' Tam backs towards the door.

'Goodbye. And bugger off.'

Tam closes the door on the sound of her laughter, a noise as if she were gargling with too little liquid.

She is sitting in a high-backed chair. Wings jut out on either side, cutting off her view. A plastic tray bearing a cup and saucer is slung between the arms of the chair. Tam knows her at once, shrunken though she is from the figure of her memory. She put a chair down in front of her and sits.

'Hello grandma.'

The blue, watered eyes regard her coldly.

'It's Tam, I've come to see you.'

'I can see who it is. Go away.'

'I've only just arrived.' Tam grins.

'Someone might see you.' She turns her head from side to side, trying to see beyond the blinkering wings, 'I don't want anyone seeing you with me.'

'Why not?' Tam smiles still, running a list of nasty words through her head.

'Where's Eileen?'

'I dunno,' Tam glances about at the serried chairs, 'at work, I expect.'

'Why hasn't she come? She never comes.'

'She's always here.'

'I suppose you've come to jeer.' Ada stirs her tea fiercely, 'Now that I'm stuck away here.'

Tam's hands dangle loosely over her knees. One foot taps the floor, a slight, controlled movement.

'I don't want you looking at me.'

'Where'd you want me to look, grandma?'

'I suppose you think I want to look at you. Feast my eyes on you, that's what you think.'

There is a short silence. Ada says, articulating the words with care as if emphasising her precision: 'You're filth, that's what you are.'

Tam rises from her chair; an easy fluid motion. Her hands catch the edge of the tray, tilting it over towards the old woman. The cup and saucer rise into the air, turning over, and the hot tea falls in a brown jet down Ada's front. The scene slows to a different time: Tam observes each drop of liquid, its precise passage through the air, the path of the cup, the slow opening of Ada's mouth in a scream.

She runs down the corridors, that twist and open into one another like the landscape of a dream. Screams of rage seem to echo down towards her. Tam runs through the doors into the street and on down the road, leaping into the air to catch at the branches of trees.

Marie inserts her feet carefully between two piles of plates on the table and leans back, folding her arms.

'What you doing tonight, Tam?'

'Same as usual.' On the bed Tam rolls over onto her back. Beverley sits hunched over the fire, head sunk between her shoulders. 'Don't bother to ask me, will you?'

'You can tell us, Tam. We're not going to give you away, are we.'

'She doesn't trust us.' Beverley picks up a fork and bounces it against the fireguard.

'Why don't you do the washing-up, Bev.'

'That's a good idea.' Marie moves her foot, pushing plates nearer the edge.

'What's the point of doing dishes on a Saturday afternoon?' They listen to the noise of Beverley's strumming.

'I can't tell you, it's undercover. The less everyone knows the safer it is.'

'Diminished responsibility.' Beverley bangs louder, slapping her other hand against her shoe.

'I'm not telling you.'

After a while the sound of the fork thins out and stops. Beverley tosses it across the carpet. A helicopter passes overhead, rattling the windows. They listen to the sound of its coming and going.

'Expect they're looking for you,' Marie flicks dust from her trousers, 'any minute now they'll crash through the window in sludgy green uniforms.'

The three of them stare ahead, waiting for a filling of the silence. The fire crackles, emitting white sparks. Tam sighs and lifts a pillow to cover her face.

'Maybe I should just suffocate myself.'

'Someone has to do it for you, stupid. How can you hold a pillow over your mouth when you're unconscious?'

'Why kill yourself when so many other people want to anyway?'

'Yeh.'

Tam puts the cushion under her head. Marie lifts her

feet from the table, careful as a cat between puddles, and walks over to the window.

'It's getting dark.' The street light shimmers on her face.

'And again we have done nothing.' Beverley throws her hands in the air and rocks backwards and forwards. She waggles her fingers, opens her mouth wide, groans. Tam watches her, laughing. Beverley clutches her chest and tosses her head from side to side. She flops sideways onto the floor holding herself, letting out the noises of a soul in despair. She and Tam roll about, gasping, kicking their legs in the air.

Marie watches them from the window, 'You're going to knock those dishes over.'

Beverley grabs the table legs and shakes. A plate frees itself from the pile and slides down on top of her, scattering knives and forks and morsels of food. She lies supine, the plate overturned on her chest. Her laughter comes in little gasps, making the plate dance.

'Horrible little piglets.'

Marie turns away, to the life of the street. On the corner a knot of men lean over something between them. If the room were silent she would be able to hear the urgency of their voices.

'Wee wee wee.'

Beverley turns her squeal into a high-pitched wailing cry, begins to turn it into a tune, the song of the piglet.

'You can't be serious, can you.' Her back is turned, but the high song rings in her head.

'You're not so serious.'

Tam leans up on her elbow to stare. Marie keeps herself away, apart, imagining herself leaning down there on the corner, her hand on a shoulder, her cool voice.

'Why don't *you* do the washing-up, anyway?'

Tam looks at the spread of grease about her, almost managing indignation. The lift of Marie's shoulders mocks her.

'Oh, her mind is on higher things.' Beverley lifts a hand, limply. Her eyes are closed, the plate rises and falls gently.

'Maybe I will do them. Before I go out.' Marie twirls round to look at them, hands on her hips. For a moment it is as if she has moved away, given them up, with their childish foolishness and warmth.

Beverley opens one eye, 'We're going together, remember? Going to hit the nightspots. The deadly sisters.'

'Maybe I go by myself.'

'Not in my dress you don't.'

Marie turns the tap in the sink violently. In the roof above them the pipes begin to shudder.

'Well, I guess there's no escape.'

Beverley grasps her plate and scrambles to her feet. She begins to dance between table and sink with plates. As she piles them beside Marie she leans toward her and warbles, a domesticated, cheerful piglet song. On Marie's other side Tam stands with a dishcloth spread between her hands, only waiting for something to dry. Marie's distance crumbles at this careful onslaught, she is reminded how necessary Bev's presence can be in the dangerous places they are going, the exciting places. How Beverley can talk her way out of anything.

'Mama gonna buy me a diamond ring,' Marie hums, forgetting herself.

Marie poses in the dress, hip slung to the side, arm behind her head. It is the dress for it, black, tight, slits here and there to give a sensation of bondage partially released.

'Well?'

'That Bev's dress?' Tam narrows her eyes.

'What of it?'

'Nothing.' Tam looks her over, 'Well, it looks like Bev's dress.' Marie comes out of the pose and runs her hands uneasily over her front, 'What do you mean?'

'She means, you don't spill out of it like I do.' Beverley stands draped in the doorway, the red of her dress around her waist: 'Billie Holliday to my Bessie Smith, that's you.'

'Shit.'

Marie dives at the cigarettes on the table. She cups a hand under her elbow. The smoke from the cigarette drifts up toward the ceiling: it is an old photograph, black and white and signed across one corner.

Tam lowers her head to her magazine. 'You look fine.'

Marie stalks away to stare at her reflection in the window-pane. Beverley shrugs herself into her dress.

Tam looks down at newsprint, not seeing it. She listens to Beverley moving about putting things on her face, to Marie sorting through her collection of shoes. She hears, acutely, the slide of nylon on leather, the dry rasp of combs struggling through hair. When she looks up, finally, they are standing in front of her, coats rustling.

Beverley flings out her arms: 'The deadly sisters hit the town!'

Tam waves, 'See you tomorrow.'

'If you're lucky.'

'Don't wake us, we won't wake you.'

They depart, slamming the door and clicking their heels on the stairs.

STREET SCENE: FIVE

Elsie is there, as always, behind the door before the scene opens. It begins only when someone arrives.

This evening there are only the four of them: Gloria, Tam, Sue, Ruth. Sheila lies bandaged, immured above the city.

Elsie lets them into her front room and closes the door on them, winged things let back into a cage.

Gloria feels her age tonight. Centuries press down on her, a grey sponge, amidst this restless, glittered youth. How wise of Elsie to have retired from active service, to have taken the desk job as if it were the true burden. It is obvious to Gloria, feeling her age thoughtfully between her hands, where the burden is tonight.

Tam looks at the bright screen behind her eyelids. It is showing in continuous replay the old people's home scenario in which she reaches forward deftly and spills the contents of her grandmother's tea tray down her front. She watches as her grandmother's dress darkens under the tea stain. How, after a fractional pause, the mouth opens and the arms begin to windmill feebly.

Sue has been having a good time today playing resident rich person again. She has been standing in chic, dim stores clad in co-ordinating underwear while perfect women bring her shimmering items of non-functional clothing. She has tried them all on, floated them about, twirled on her heel, looked at herself in the mirror until she can see nothing else. She has bought several things, imagining the various nightclubs in which she might make a seductive spectacle. Maybe she will just tear herself limb from limb, have done with it all.

This afternoon Ruth had the telephone call for which she has been waiting such a long time. He breathed, Sadie said, and the breathing filled the whole house with its noise, and then he stopped. Ruth is thinking about the magnolia, what it will do now, having been poised for so long, will it flower or crumple?

Elsie, watching them all in, suppresses as not useful her sense of the futility of their efforts. Now is not the time to question the basis on which they do what they do. If it seems to her increasingly an attempt at hastening their own destruction, perhaps she had better take them aside one at a time, or perhaps she had better stand apart and let them do as they will.

'They didn't get you?' Tam asks, looking at Sue, unblemished and glowing.

'I ran. Sheila told me to.'

Tam pours herself a cup of coffee from the pot, brimful: liquid as a weapon.

'And you always do what she says.'

Sue lines herself up with the door.

'I thought she was running too.'

Tam drinks, eyeing her over the rim, 'We all make mistakes.'

Gloria climbs out of her chair, placing her body, solid, between them.

'We could go somewhere else tonight, Tam. Somewhere altogether different.'

Tam lifts her eyes, 'With you, I'm altogether different.'

They leave abruptly, making a sudden space in the room. Sue has backed herself against the wall. Ruth waits, suspended.

'Maybe you shouldn't go out tonight.'

They recognize the voice of sanity and begin at once to gather themselves together, pulling on gloves, putting down cups, checking their pockets for identifying papers. They know that it is necessary to act in concert, or they will be stopped. Made to listen, made to drink tea and reveal themselves.

'I'll look after Sue.' Ruth grins ambiguously.

'Don't you worry about us, Elsie.'

They stand briefly together in the doorway, as if framed for a portrait. Elsie only looks at them from the middle of the room, coffee pot held in front of her.

Later that evening Elsie comes to the decision that she will clean the front room thoroughly. Something that, after all, she does too infrequently. It is, she tells herself, as good a way as any of passing the time. In the early hours of the morning the room looks as if she is moving out unexpectedly, with no time to pack properly and no expectation of return. It is an unnecessary reminder of the fragility of her hold on the ordinary fabric of life. She begins to put everything hurriedly back in its place, perhaps in the hope that no notice has been taken of her exposure.

They are walking a little too fast as if someone were about to call them back. Ruth lays her hand on Sue's sleeve and Sue starts. They both stop, then, look at one another sideways and begin to walk again in careful step.

'It wasn't that I was frightened.'

'No.'

'I'm just well-drilled. She does always tell me what to do.'

'That is Sheila's way.'

Ruth wonders whether perhaps she should visit, offer to buy groceries. She cannot imagine herself making the effort.

'Have you been to see her,' she asks, 'I expect she understands.'

'She might just batter me with her crutch.'

Ruth laughs explosively, reeling along the midnight railings.

'It feels funny being here.'

Tam shovels food into her mouth. All the burners are on against the cold and the oven is open into the room, its wide lip threatening to burn someone's chair in the crush.

'Funny you haven't been before. I don't know where Gloria's been keeping you.'

Grace has the ladle poised over her plate again.

'Oh, in my pocket and places.'

Tammy focuses on the food that appears on her plate, so much of it, the variety and endlessness of it, the sing-song half-words of encouragement that go with it. She can feel the nourishment pushing its way along her body, shovelling into the toes, clearing a pathway into the brain, obliterating so much. She smiles around her fork.

'You get a lot out of watching her eat, don't you?'

Gloria says. Like one of those nativity tableaus, this scene, glowing colours and a hushed gaze on the centre of events, worship the food for it is our daily comfort. Gloria gets up from the table, 'Maybe I'll go out and find Joe, as you're managing so well without me.'

'I expect he'll fall over with surprise, you not prowling those streets tonight.'

'Not only from that, I dare say.'

Gloria lets the street door slam behind her. Grace and Tam do not lift their heads.

Sheila lies on her side watching the orange glow of the city. In the spaces between breaths she can almost fall into sleep, before the rising of her ribs stabs her awake. Somewhere else, behind her, something is aching steadily, peaceable so long as she keeps still. Only if she were to think of moving would it snap into life, bite into her back. The cat has curled itself carefully beside her stomach, a small irrelevant lump of warmth. It is lying low, the survival strategy that has worked before.

Ruth walks close, letting her shoulder touch Sue's. As they walk through the shopping precinct the lighted windows throw their shadows, etiolated and sharp, across the tarmac. They have the look of stalking spirits stepping effortless across the waste.

Ahead of them, people are spilling out onto the pavement. As they come near, music, half-heard, is silenced. Ruth and Sue move forward smoothly, their limbs well-oiled and unfaltering, too automatic to stop.

Before they have entirely noticed, there is a crowd around them. Only a small crowd, and swaying gently from the effects of the music, cocktails, shifting from foot to foot on a floor that vibrates, making your legs shake for hours afterwards. Ruth makes to go on, as if she had not noticed them. She hardly has; they are inconsequential to her desire to walk smoothly beside Sue down slick, dark streets, feeling the blood in her veins. She takes another step; another and she will have glided between them and passed on.

Sue sees them in front of her very clearly, young men in dancing costume. She might easily be with them, tomorrow, choosing one or other because she likes the shape of his head, or the way he bites his nails. They have no call to be here, when it is someone else she is being.

'Get out of my way.'

She comes to a dead stop, waiting for them to fall back.

Something about her tone engages them: they look down at her, see the two women for the first time. Their interest, deadened by noise and dancing, is unleashed. They step a little closer, make cheerful, teasing comments. One reaches out as if to put his arm about her.

Ruth pulls at Sue's arm; she can see the way forward so clearly. Sue only shrugs her off. She opens her mouth and begins to shout, a stream of abuse. They fall back, discomforted.

In the ringing silence Sue goes on standing in the middle of the circle that has formed round her. Soon they will be angry, ashamed of not having retaliated.

'Time to go, Sue.'

Ruth starts off towards the outside, glancing over her shoulder to see Sue start to move with her.

'Run, can't you?'

Instead, Ruth sees Sue moving round the circle, her arms and legs snapping out at them. She hears sharp sounds, gasps, the crumpling of cloth.

This can continue for a short time only. Eventually the sleepy young men must master their surprise and think to retaliate, so many of them as there are.

'You think I'm going to run again?' Sue laughs, lashing out. Ruth abandons herself to the task then, gladly enough. They are unco-ordinated and tired and she feels fresh, unused. She begins to pick them off from behind. Each kick, and the small intake of breath as they stagger and feel for the hurt, is more a pleasure than otherwise.

It takes her a moment to identify the knife; it seems to her to be taking things more seriously than is necessary.

He is inexpert, carries a weapon rather for display

than use: he likes to think it warns off troublemakers. The small crouching figure moving from foot to foot outside his reach unnerves him slightly, but he feels invincible with the knife clasped firmly in his hand.

The look of surprise as she kicks his wrist reminds Ruth of some other time, a memory that she cannot place. The knife skitters across the pavement.

Sue is on the ground, fighting blindly. She can hear the guttural sound she is still making, and feel the jerks as something hard kicks into her side. She closes her teeth on flesh and hears a new high note of pain.

Ruth picks up the knife. She remembers, as her fingers curl round the handle, the connection she needed. It is of him, of course. Sitting propped up against so many pillows. The look of surprise and shock, a refusal to comprehend, as he tried to lift a cup unaided and the liquid teetered and spilled away from him, dropping from his hand. The same incomprehension, the end of a lifetime of unquestionable strength.

Ruth launches herself so lightly towards him. He really should not have looked like that, made it seem so humane, to end his misery. There is also the question of retribution, you for him, who suffered unnecessarily. It is better that someone should have their just deserts. A life for a life. As the knife goes in he screams, an extreme sound, unmistakeable. Ruth lies on top of him feeling the juddering and twitching of his body. She feels a great relief, that he does not have to breathe anymore, uttering that wracking, painful gasp.

They have fled, at that awful high-pitched sound. Sue gets to her feet. It is Ruth that she expects to see, laid out on the ground. Instead Ruth is kneeling beside him, holding his hand.

'Your heart was too strong, I had to stop it.'

She wipes her eyes, smearing blood across her face.

'I think we should go now. He's dead, anyway.'

Ruth seems to be calm. Sue removes her blood-stained jacket and wipes her hands and face on a handkerchief. When told to go home to bed she starts off in the right direction as if glad to be told what is appropriate. Sue takes the jacket and the knife down to the canal. As she walks she begins to feel her bruises.

ELSEWHERE: FOUR

After each session with the weights A covers herself with oil, a particular kind that was passed to her at a fete when she had unexpectedly shot down the row of tin ducks (and a bullet to spare which, that day, she had not been concerned to use).

The oil makes her glow externally, a strange radiance that disconcerts passers-by on the street. They glance again but covertly for fear of her stare. They look and tell themselves it is her skin type that produces an unearthly radiance. If they are of a similar colour, and hopeful, they may go home and experiment with the cooking oil.

A is only peripherally concerned with the effects of her action, though she is not unsympathetic to the idea of the young seeking to emulate her; it may be a step in the right direction. A's attention is concentrated on the perfection of herself, the achievement of herself as a suitable instrument. The social desirability of this plan is not universally acknowledged, which requires that A keep her activities to some extent veiled from the public gaze. Thus she presents herself as being in pursuit of physical strength, as being obsessed by the expandable limits of bodily capacity – heart or lungs, say, speed of reactions, or the possibilities of co-ordination. Accordingly she enters contests of an athletic or sporting nature, restraining her success rate to a level which ensures her ease of entry to those places where she might wish to go. She is careful not to approximate to a standard that might be perceived by others as superhuman. A is concerned to evoke no serious comment or detailed analysis of her activities. It is also necessary that she not attract, at this stage, too many eager disciples.

Superficially, the external details of A's life are peculiar – it is thus that she successfully conceals herself. Watching the record of an endurance test, A holed up above the tree line without visible means of protection, viewers are encouraged to dwell upon the eccentricity of her daily habits. The things that she does – whether preparatory with weights, say, or actual, with guns or stamina – seem obviously only attainable by an excessive form of devotion. They do not see their own way of life as threatened by something so clearly beyond and other than what a normal person might be prepared to undertake. It is a measure of A's success that they do not ask themselves why she considers her self-training worthwhile; they accept that the pleasure of achievement can be enough in itself. Watchers do not, therefore, penetrate to A's hidden motivation, or to a sense of what truly renders her way of life an aberration.

For many years, A is to be seen in the pursuit of excellence. Only the most alert could wonder at the slight twitch of the lip with which she receives some passing medal, at the carriage of her body as she strides off a field, carving her way through the crowd. On a particular day, the weights put aside, the body anointed, A goes out into the city square, her head covered as those of women are at this season. She chooses a bench at the centre, near the fountain. She concentrates herself upon those who are strolling near her, listening to the sound of the water, feeling the afternoon sun on their faces, considering the clothes of those around them. She finds that she can readily tune into their conversations; it is only hard to differentiate between what she is picking up directly in her mind and the snatches that she hears by ordinary means. A explores the facility only briefly, restraining herself from further experimentation. Later, her methods perfected so that she may obtain the same results with the expenditure of minimal energy, A uses this additional technique to advantage in her competitive activities. A has no concept of the fair or sacred; it is axiomatic to her that any means may be employed to a given end.

The crucial second stage of A's plan is reached when A has acquired, through an unremitting dedication, the necessary skills to allow her to do with herself and those around her as she wishes. It is at this point that A is called upon to decide which of two rather different paths to take. She has available to her the means of influencing others: either she could enable the common herd to attain a similar skill, with a view to allowing each individual to change the world on their own behalf, or she might simply bring her own influence to bear on those chiefly in control in such a way that through her direct intervention the necessary changes are made.

A is not entirely confident in her own judgement; on the other hand she is not quite trusting of the judgement of others. She allows herself a few days during which to consider the options. Seeking for distraction rather than concentration, she enters herself for one of the marathon contests that the country has lately taken up with enthusiasm.

The game requires that contestants run from the northern tip of the continent to its western border, without sleep or solid food. In the early stages of the race small friendly crowds gather by the roadside waving tree branches against the heat and holding out cups of nourishing broth to the contestants. A few villagers join in with the leaders for a spell; others run beside the stragglers, telling them stories to keep them awake. A, her head uncovered and her body glistening with oil, runs smoothly along with the pack, listening to the stories, smiling at the children, drinking the proffered refreshments. Some of the girls climb trees and throw down petals into her hair.

As the day wears on into evening the runners pass into the high mountain region of the north. For hours they run between pine trees, their feet shuffling through thick beds of needles. A few begin to pause, to turn aside or sink down between the trees with slackened faces. These regions are populated only in high summer; here the runners are alone, to journey on or not, as they choose.

When the dawn breaks there are seen to be fewer of them. They are running now across the industrial plain, the streets choked with dust carts and delivery vehicles. A few people stop to stare on their way to work, or lean, curious, out of windows. In the centre of the city there will be a relief station, refreshment booths and first aid; they run on at a steady pace.

At the refreshment stop they are providing a balanced

liquid feed: it tastes of salt and most contestants are unable to drink it down. A crowd has gathered to cheer them on. They soon realise that the nutritious soup is unpalatable and urge the runners to drink it, laughing when they gag, greeting a successful gulp with bursts of ironical applause. A drinks a cupful and throws the empty container into the throng. Someone catches it and hides it under her shirt, a trophy.

That night, running through the countryside, two runners bringing up the rear are hit by a truck. When the news spreads up the line those at the front slow down until they are all running together, as a pack. Their feet make a sudden noise on the cobbles as they pass through darkened villages. As they travel towards the west the weather breaks; it begins to rain, and a wet scudding wind blows into their faces. In the morning they are running across moors, a light mist seeping across the landscape. The refreshment booth is missing, set up on the wrong road a mile or so across the moor. When the mistake is rectified the runners are long gone. As they run they suck the moisture from their clothes and chew sprigs of heather, earthy and bitter.

A runs lightly beside them. It is not the fittest who have survived, she observes, but rather those who are able to detach themselves from mundane physical process. A considers the possibility that their motivation is larger than it appears, but in their thoughts she finds only the abstractions of self-knowledge.

The land narrows towards the western border; for a time they are almost within sight of the sea. They hear a brass band playing, faintly, and pass a crowd of people in a field, looking up into the sky. Later a refreshment station appears around a bend in the road, manned by children in blue uniforms. The drink they offer is sweetish and bubbly; some of the runners stop to drink again, the flavour of it intoxicating. When they start off once more some of the children run ahead in tight formation. As they run they sing; snatches of a tune come back to the runners, mocking, high voices singing of heroic deeds, of days long gone.

It is their final night: they will reach the border as dawn comes. As the light fades in front of them a few runners turn aside, singly or in pairs, as if unwilling to face what lies ahead. They turn away , towards the sea. As the night wears on the runners begin to speak to one another, to discuss how they will cross the line, who will be there to meet them. They make jokes about how the finishing line will be on the other side, and they have not brought their passports. A listens, wondering at this camaraderie that comes from nowhere, that will end with a piece of tape stretched across an arbitrary space. She wonders at their dissipation of energy, at the uncritical affection that they feel for themselves, for her, for the heedless landscape through which they pass.

They break the tape in the dead hour before dawn, a noisy crowd, their arms in the air, laughing and shouting. The race officials are half-awake, listless, impatient for sleep. The reporters cannot decide who has won; the runners say they all want to be interviewed together, that they have all come first. They stand about, sharing blankets and cups of some nameless drink. After an hour or so a few runners begin to collapse, sinking quietly to the ground, their eyes glazing over. A stands apart, watching, as the reporters pack their microphones and leave, as the finishing tape is rewound into a leather bag and the officials pile into their cars, throwing clipboards into the back seats. Soon there is no one left save a knot of runners, huddled in their blankets and, across an acre of rough ground, the dim orange lights of the border post.

A moves into the centre of the group and looks round: what now, she asks. A few of them shrug, or close their eyes as if the question were irrelevant. One of them says, finally, that they don't know the answer to that, but that perhaps they will rest. I can run back now, A says, and if you want, you may come with me. I know what you're thinking, she says, precisely. If you come with me now, I will teach you everything. The runners look at her listlessly. The point of this is power, A continues, don't you want to take a hand in the world? Come back with me, and then you may use it as you see fit. I won't interfere. They are silent, leaning wearily together. I could use my powers of persuasion, she says, and you would be unable to resist. But I am giving you the opportunity to choose. Otherwise I shall go and do it myself. A pauses, looking round at them. Because you are so very inexperienced I will give you a few minutes to think about it. And then I am going to run back. Because sooner or later, the process must begin. A leaves the circle and goes to stand in the roadway, her face to the east, the way they have come.

The runners look at one another, rousing themselves to a final effort. Is this what we want, they ask each other, can this be what we intended? She has not given us any details, someone remarks, this is the vaguest of offers, and shrouded in threats and unreal choices. But perhaps it is necessary to have faith, they argue. It is true that she ran easier, more lightly than the rest of us, a woman says, as if she were not quite earthbound, but is that significant? Is she making us an offer that we cannot refuse, that is the question. They laugh, seeing the impenetrable nature of their difficulty.

They cross the roadway to where she stands. Someone picks a handful of berries from a bush. All right then, they say, we will come with you. But don't forget it's we who are doing you a favour. And if you're so good at this, let's see a refreshment booth every few miles this time, and on the right road. A looks at them, you will have to take me seriously, she says, I can do anything. Maybe, they say, so where is that light nourishing meal that we all need so much? A smiles and points down the road. Round a few bends, she says, such things take a little time to prepare. As the dawn come up they set off, leaving the grass behind then strewn with fallen blankets.

THE FOREGROUND

Gloria sits by Ruth's bed, holding her hand. It looks like she doesn't have time to find someone to hold her own.

'He was some no-account. And you didn't know what you were doing, did you.'

Gloria is clear that this is self-indulgence. You can't afford to let yourself go like that. But she lies easily, with hardly a flicker of an eyelid, at Ruth's need.

'Nobody's going to miss him, kid, are they?'

Even for Ruth, surely, things are not that simple. Gloria rubs her fingers in her eyes: 'Want something to drink?'

Ruth considers, watching the flicker of yellow street light on the ceiling. She remembers that he used, as a young man, to poach rabbits in the long evenings of summer. Jogging over the short grass of the downs, dog at his heels. A gentleman may poach the odd rabbit, and sleep easy. There are rules that the individual, trusting himself, may overstep.

He was eager to have done; to be away from indignity. She only lent him the strength he lacked, to do it himself. She has seen him kill a sick bird, stroke its feathers gently and twist the neck. It was a skill he meant to pass on, surely.

She takes the cup Gloria holds out: 'I did the right thing.'

Gloria goes home across town in the reluctant light of morning. She who is not free to be irresponsible, who must more than account for each action. Weighed down now by this, by another's freedom.

She stops at a café, finding her knees suddenly shaking under her. From behind the counter the woman eyes her, it never lets up. Skilfully she slops tea into the saucer, leaves the sugar out of reach. This is what she gets up for, seven days out of seven, to serve the likes of Gloria with tea.

Gloria hunches over her cup. In her mind the list of

those she could so well strike down, and in righteous anger. So many whose evil is apparent, who would crush the life out of her if they could. And yet she has held back, has tried to believe that it is not necessary to descend to their level, to exact vengeance. And now even her rage has been used, taken and used; frittered in an alley by some half-awake spoilt child.

Gloria stirs another spoonful of sugar into her tea-cup and swears steadily, soft but clear, curses Ruth and all like her into oblivion.

The woman behind the counter draws her lips into a thin white line; it is what she would expect.

Elsie keeps the curtains drawn while the fire burns. The newspaper cuttings curl into wide flakes and float out of the grate. The rug is littered with details of violence, half-burnt. The notes of where she found her protagonists, the meetings and bars, the addresses of houses she insinuated herself into, looking for a certain desperation: all these burn easily, disappearing with conspiratorial suddenness. She watches the anthropological data dissolve forever without fear; it would only have been misinterpreted. Elsie's lingering wish for a history, an abiding knowledge of the struggle, goes up with the flames.

In the bathroom mirror she sees that she has singed her hair. She clips away with the scissors; they will have to start over. It will be no loss to be clear of this randomness. It is an opportunity to decide at last who are the true targets. Elsie grins at herself in the mirror, coming clean as a terrorist at last.

On the canal path Sue walks slowly, the parcel folded to her chest. Beneath the dry rustle of layers of newspaper she can sense the stickiness of blood, thick clots in the jacket's folds. It is hours she has been walking; soon enough the winter dawn will catch her, still walking triumphant along the path.